D0174844

Match Wits with The Hardy Boys®!

Collect the Original
Hardy Boys Mystery Stories®

by Franklin W. Dixon

Celebrate 60 Years with the World's Greatest Super Sleuths!

MYSTERY OF THE DESERT GIANT

"That dust devil will wreck our plane!"

The Hardy Boys Mystery Stories®

MYSTERY

OF THE

DESERT GIANT

BY

FRANKLIN W. DIXON

GROSSET & DUNLAP
Publishers • New York
A member of The Putnam & Grosset Group

PRINTED ON RECYCLED PAPER

Copyright © 1989, 1961 by Simon & Schuster, Inc. All rights reserved.
Published by Grosset & Dunlap, Inc., a member of The Putnam &
Grosset Group, New York. Published simultaneously in Canada. Printed in the U.S.A.
THE HARDY BOYS® is a registered trademark of Simon & Schuster, Inc.
GROSSET & DUNLAP is a trademark of Grosset & Dunlap, Inc.
ISBN 0-448-08940-8
2002 Printing

CONTENTS

CHAPTER I

Missing Airmen

"WHEN do you think this mysterious visitor is going to show up?" Chet Morton asked impatiently.

The chubby boy looked uncomfortable as he squatted behind a waist-high hedge. Chet's companions, Joe and Frank Hardy, who were experienced campers, rested easily upon their haunches.

"Can't say," replied Frank Hardy in a low but distinct voice. "The person on the phone said to beware of the man who's calling at our house tonight. And he didn't give his name or that of the man who's coming here to see Dad."

The trio had taken their positions shortly after dark. From their hiding places they commanded a view of the front walk of the Hardy home in Bayport.

"I checked with Mother and Aunt Gertrude. They aren't expecting anyone," Joe Hardy said

1

thoughtfully. "And Dad had an appointment on the other side of town tonight—"

"But," put in Frank, the older of the two brothers, "the man on the phone said the Hardys had better watch their step! That's why we want you to take a picture of him, Chet, with that new infrared camera of yours."

"Here we go again," the stout boy moaned. "Can't you Hardys solve your mysteries without me? All I ever get out of your cases is bruises!"

At that moment a sharp jab in the ribs by Joe alerted the others. The quick scrape of leather on concrete could be heard out front. Abruptly, the footsteps stopped.

Peering, the boys made out the indistinct figure of a man who had just turned into the Hardy walk. The man stood motionless for a moment, then the boys heard his footsteps dying away down High Street.

"Changed his mind," commented Frank, puzzled. "What's going on here?"

"We'll find out! I got his picture!" Chet cried out.

"Hush!" Frank cautioned. "He may not have been *the* visitor."

As he spoke, the boys heard more footsteps. This time they were the strong, confident steps of a man who entered the walk and strode purposefully toward the Hardys' front door. Simultaneously, Mr. Hardy's car turned into the driveway.

As Chet snapped the man's picture, Joe debated whether to tell his father immediately about the telephone message. He decided against it. Leaving now would give away their position and ruin the element of surprise.

"Let's go!" Frank Hardy signaled.

Abruptly the three boys broke through the hedge into the path of the astonished caller.

"*Who* are you?" Chet burst out.

"Why, I'm Philip Dodge—I've come to see Mr. Fenton Hardy, the investigator. We have an appointment tonight."

"I beg your pardon, Mr. Dodge," Frank apologized. "We thought you might be—another visitor." He introduced himself and the others.

"We'll take you in to Dad," Joe volunteered, leading the way. "He just arrived home."

As Joe and the visitor entered the house, Frank whispered to Chet, "Why not develop your pictures while Dad talks to Mr. Dodge? The lab is open. I'm curious to see who our first visitor was—I'm also wondering if Dodge is the man we were warned about."

"Great idea!"

Carrying his camera, Chet disappeared around the house. He liked nothing better than to putter in the well-equipped laboratory the Hardy boys had built on the second floor of their garage. More than once the lab had been useful to them in their detective work.

Meanwhile, the brothers ushered their visitor into the comfortably furnished Hardy living room. In the light of the room the contrast between serious-minded Frank Hardy and impetuous Joe was apparent. Eighteen-year-old Frank was dark-haired and Joe, a year younger, fair-haired.

As their father greeted Mr. Dodge, whom he seemed to know well, the boys turned to go. Fenton Hardy, a tall, broad-shouldered man in his forties, held up his hand.

"Hold it, boys! No reason you shouldn't hear this. I've a hunch you'll find it interesting. You don't object, do you, Phil?"

"No. Of course not."

Frank and Joe needed no second invitation. Mr. Hardy and his sons took seats, while Philip Dodge stood nervously by the fireplace. He was a well-dressed, middle-aged man.

"Fenton, I've never been so baffled in my life!" he burst out. "As a lawyer, I've had some odd cases. But this time I'm up against a brick wall!

"I have an office here in Bayport, boys. Not long ago a retired manufacturer, Clement H. Brownlee, came to me and asked if I would try to locate his nephew. It seems this nephew, Willard Grafton, had been a highly successful young industrialist in Los Angeles. About three months ago he disappeared!"

"How did he disappear?" Fenton Hardy asked.

"Well, he liked to fly his own plane on business trips around the country," the lawyer resumed. "Three months ago he and a friend named Clifford Wetherby took off on a flight over the California desert, near the Colorado River. Since then, nobody has seen a trace of Willard Grafton *or* Clifford Wetherby!"

The visitor's bafflement was apparent as he paced up and down the room. In contrast, Fenton Hardy's manner was calm and professional.

"What about the plane? They don't usually just vanish, Phil."

"The plane—oh, the plane was found all right. It had been landed, very neatly, too, on the desert near a bluff about sixteen miles north of the town of Blythe, California."

"Anything wrong with the plane?" Joe asked.

"Low on fuel, but not damaged otherwise. That's what really baffles me. It looks as if Grafton set his ship down on that desert deliberately."

"Grafton and Wetherby must have walked away," Joe stated. "But where?"

"There wasn't a trace showing where they went or what had happened," Mr. Dodge said.

"You've notified the local police, of course, and have had the area searched thoroughly?" Mr. Hardy queried.

"Oh, yes, Mr. Brownlee saw to that before he consulted me. No results. No evidence that the men had died, and no leads to their whereabouts.

The Air Force even supplied an Air Rescue team to help in the search, but nothing turned up. I went out there and flew over the area myself last week, but I didn't learn anything, either."

While Philip Dodge was speaking, Frank Hardy sat quietly in his chair. Something in the lawyer's story jogged his memory. "You say this plane was landed in the desert above Blythe, California? Near the Colorado River?"

"That's right."

"Shall I tell you what I think you saw below you?"

"All right—shoot."

"You saw giants on the desert. Giants better than a hundred feet tall."

"Giants!" burst from the bewildered Joe Hardy and his father.

"You guessed it, Frank." Mr. Dodge chuckled. Fenton Hardy looked from his visitor to his elder son. "This sounds a little like a private joke."

Philip Dodge laughed. "Maybe you'd better explain, Frank. By the way, how did you know?"

"The name Blythe stuck in my mind," the young man admitted. "Joe and I read a lot when we're not busy on a case. Some time last year I came across information on the desert giants.

"As I understand it, a few hundred years ago the Indians around the California-Arizona border drew a number of huge pictures on the desert surfaces. The giant on the Arizona side of the

Colorado River opposite Blythe, California, is one of the biggest of all."

Joe Hardy laughed. "Whew! What kind of pencil do you use to draw pictures that size?"

"The Indians scraped away the surface gravel in very shallow furrows. The hard soil underneath gave them distinct tan-colored lines for their pictures."

"It doesn't make much sense to me," Joe objected. "The Indians drew pictures better than a hundred feet tall on the desert. What for? How could they even *see* their pictures, once they were drawn?"

"I guess that's a mystery in itself," Philip Dodge commented.

But suddenly Frank broke in once more.

"Joe's got something!" he announced. "It's true, the only way to see the desert giants is from the air. The Indians couldn't see them, but *we can!*"

"I see what you're getting at, Frank," Fenton Hardy said excitedly. "You mean the various giant figures were visible to Willard Grafton and Clifford Wetherby as they flew over the desert?"

"And they landed their plane to have a closer look!" Joe finished eagerly.

"Maybe that's the answer to your first question, Mr. Dodge."

The lawyer, however, was not satisfied. "These

scratch marks don't mean anything, Fenton. I wouldn't have mentioned them myself, if Frank hadn't reminded me. Why, once you're on the ground, you can't see them at all!"

"That makes them all the more valuable as possible clues to the lost men," the experienced investigator answered. "In detective work, sometimes it's the crazy clues that bring results. This case is really beginning to interest me."

"Then you'll help me find Grafton?" the visitor asked eagerly.

Fenton Hardy hesitated. The international reputation he had won since leaving the New York City Police Department to become a private investigator in Bayport had brought more cases to him than he could accept.

"Phil, I'm afraid I can't possibly leave the case I'm engaged on now." When their visitor expressed his disappointment, the detective added, "However, if you agree, I can start my two chief assistants on the case."

"Wonderful!" Philip Dodge brightened. "When may I talk with them?"

"Immediately. They happen to be seated right here in this room."

Puzzled, the lawyer looked around. Then he understood. "Really, Fenton. I have heard about some of Frank's and Joe's adventures. But do you think this case can be entrusted to amateurs?"

"Frank and Joe are amateurs, but very experienced," said their father proudly. "Recently they broke up a gang of international air-freight thieves, with practically no assistance from me. What do you say they fly out to Blythe and look things over, at least until I can get on the case myself?"

Much to the elation of the brothers, Philip Dodge agreed.

"Hurray! Let's tell Chet!" Joe urged. "Where is he, anyway? It doesn't take this long to develop pictures."

"Developing pictures—ha-ha! Probably he came in the back way and stopped first for a piece of cake in the kitchen," Frank answered.

But good-natured Chet Morton, who loved to eat, was not in the kitchen. In the Hardys' garage laboratory, a short while before, he had developed and printed the two pictures taken with his infrared camera. What he discovered when he examined the second print made him give an excited yelp. Chet grabbed both prints, dashed down the stairs, out of the garage, and across the yard.

Heavy darkness enveloped the whole yard and back of the house. Chet yanked at the back door, but it was locked. Running, stumbling a little in the dark, he sped around to the front entrance.

Before he reached it, something seemed to explode all at once at the back of his head. Chet felt the cool grass come up and hit his face. Then he lapsed into unconsciousness.

CHAPTER II

The Desert Giants

"Boy, it's dark tonight!" exclaimed Joe, after the brothers had walked with Mr. Dodge to the front porch and made arrangements to come to his office the next day.

"Won't make any difference to Chet's infrared camera," Frank replied. "Let's see what's on his films."

From where they stood the boys could see the light in the laboratory window. Knowing every inch of the ground, they started for the garage on the double.

Joe, who was in the lead, tripped over something and sprawled headlong. Recovering his balance with a near somersault, he called back, "Wow! What was that?"

"Chet!" cried the amazed Frank, stooping down. "He's been slugged."

Supporting the heavy, limp form of Chet Morton between them, Frank and Joe re-entered the living room. Exclamations of alarm and concern filled the house as the other members of the Hardy family came on the run.

Laura Hardy, the boys' slim and attractive mother, quickly brought cold towels and spirits of ammonia, while her husband loosened the unfortunate Chet's clothing and chafed his wrists.

Aunt Gertrude, Fenton Hardy's unmarried sister, clucked in concern. "I knew it! I knew it! This is what comes of meddling with mysteries!"

Nevertheless, Aunt Gertrude herself, a tall, angular woman of great vigor, took charge. She soaked a gauze pad in the spirits of ammonia and passed it expertly, not too close, under Chet's nose. As the pungent fumes reached his nostrils, the boy gave a sudden start and moaned.

"Whew!" The entire Hardy family breathed in relief, and Joe, to test Chet's mental state, said, "Chet! Aunt Gertrude has just baked a fresh chocolate cake!"

The stout boy roused himself still further. "D-did you say chocolate cake?" he asked weakly.

Completely aroused by this time, Chet was bombarded with questions, but could only say, "Don't ask me who did it. There I was, rushing to find you two—when *biff*, I saw stars."

"But why would anyone hit poor Chet?" asked Mrs. Hardy.

"Because he was helping the Hardy boys on a

mystery again, that's all," answered Chet with great sympathy for himself. "I had just made an important discovery."

"The pictures!" Frank and Joe exclaimed.

Chet nodded. "The first one—the fellow who went away—was just some man. I don't know who. The other one I snapped fast, and my aim wasn't too good. I didn't get much of Mr. Dodge. *But I got the full face of somebody crouching in the bushes under your living-room window!*"

"Great mackerel!" cried Joe, rummaging in his friend's pockets. "Let's see those pictures!"

To the Hardys' dismay, both prints were missing. Chet smiled. "You can always take a look at the copies I left in the lab."

"Better get them now, boys," Fenton Hardy suggested. "We must find out if the person who slugged Chet is someone interested in the case I'm working on, or the Grafton case. The picture may help to identify the prowler."

The brothers hurried to the laboratory. To their surprise and dismay the place was a shambles—it was evident that someone had made a hurried search. As the boys quickly straightened the equipment, they found no sign of the other set of prints which Chet had mentioned.

"That settles it," said Joe. "The thief doubled back after striking Chet to get any other prints and the negatives."

"Now we can't possibly identify him," Frank

moaned. A moment later he whistled. "Look!"

Tacked to the wall at the end of the laboratory was a small hastily printed note:

HARDYS BEWARE!

Beneath the note was a crude stick drawing of a man with an arrow aimed toward his heart.

"Not much of an artist, is he?" Joe mused. "Say, Frank, what does this remind you of?"

"By stretching the imagination I'd say that the figure *could* be the outline of a desert giant with an Indian arrow pointing to his heart."

"If only we hadn't lost the pictures!" Joe sighed.

"You can always print another set." Chet grinned. "I hid the negatives in that secret compartment of your workbench. What kind of a detective do you think I am, anyway?"

Frank and Joe applauded Chet's action and hurried to make prints from the negatives. Then, returning to the house, the Hardys and Chet held a brief council. None of them knew the dark-haired, muscular eavesdropper or the slender, gray-haired man who had started to turn into the Hardys' walk.

"The unknown eavesdropper," Frank said, "probably heard everything that was said to Mr. Dodge. Why did he come, unless he's connected with Willard Grafton's disappearance?"

"And with the mysterious telephone call," Joe added. Briefly, he told his father of the warning.

"What I say is this," broke in peppery Aunt Gertrude. "That terrible man outside heard you boys discussing some new mystery, and he hit poor Chet on the head to warn you to keep out of it!"

"Why, Aunt Gertrude," Joe teased with a straight face, "we're only going to take a quiet vacation in sunny California."

"*I* know how quiet it will be," snapped their aunt. "Just one danger after another."

Calm, sensible Mrs. Hardy worried a little too, but she had implicit faith in her sons' ability to take care of themselves. "Just be careful," she cautioned.

The next morning Fenton Hardy and the boys drove to police headquarters, in downtown Bayport, with the pictures. The detective had always worked closely with the police, and this had earned him the respect and friendship of Chief Ezra Collig.

"Humph. No trouble about this one," grunted the husky chief as he examined the picture of the visitor who had changed his mind and walked away from the Hardys' house. "He's Charles Blakely, trustee of the Bayport Savings Bank, and one of our fine citizens. Probably he didn't know your neighborhood and mistook your house for another one. But this fellow in the bushes looks like a mean customer. We'll have to check the rogues' gallery on him."

The picture was compared to those in the police files, but without results.

"Tough luck, boys," their father said. "And now I must hurry back to my own case."

He left them and the boys went to Mr. Dodge's office. The lawyer introduced them to a tall, bald-headed man wearing a conservative gray suit.

"Clement Brownlee, boys. Willard Grafton's uncle."

Mr. Brownlee's face grew serious as the brothers described the attack on Chet Morton. "Boys," he began with feeling, "I've no right to expose you to any danger on my nephew's account. Perhaps we'd better drop the case."

"We can't quit now, Mr. Brownlee We're making progress!" Joe protested. "Don't you see, the attack proves your nephew didn't just wander off in the desert and get lost? He is in the hands of somebody who doesn't want him found."

"This fellow," Frank added, producing the photograph.

Both men examined the picture eagerly, but to Frank's and Joe's disappointment, they ended by shaking their heads. "A complete stranger. But we'll let you know if anything turns up," the lawyer promised.

Frank and Joe spent the next day making plans and packing for the trip.

"Sunglasses and wide-brimmed hats," said Joe,

checking these articles. "The sun will be broiling hot. And canteens, also."

"Take warm clothes, too," his brother warned. "The desert nights are plenty cool."

The following morning Joe jumped out of bed singing "California, here we come!"

Mrs. Hardy and Aunt Gertrude gave the boys a hearty farewell breakfast of steak and hash-browned potatoes.

"Where's Dad?" Frank asked.

"Out before breakfast on his own mystery," Aunt Gertrude replied tartly. "Such a household!"

After breakfast Joe telephoned Chet Morton at his farm a mile outside Bayport. "Ready?"

"I was just thinking," the chubby boy said in a worried voice. "Suppose that guy who conked me is out there? I don't want to be knocked out again."

"What's he talking about, Joe?" Frank said impatiently.

"I think he's a little scared," Joe answered loud enough for Chet to hear, and with a wink at Frank.

"Say, I am not," Chet protested. "I can't wait to get out West and try some of that Mexican food!"

An hour later the three friends met at the airport and walked to the trim, blue six-seater monoplane which Fenton Hardy had purchased recently. Lean, tanned Jack Wayne, who was Mr.

Hardy's pilot, had given Frank and Joe flying lessons. Now Frank would pilot the plane to California.

"We'll tune her up, and she'll be ready to go," Jack greeted them.

Meanwhile, Chet stowed the baggage in the fuselage, finding a special place for his infrared camera. When he had filed his flight plan, Frank started the engine to taxi out for take-off.

Joe's keen eyes spotted a powerful car speeding up the road to the airport. "Hold it, Frank! I think Dad's coming."

Frank cut the engine as the detective hurried out to the plane.

"Glad I caught you, boys! I've been on the go since dawn—uncovered one of the neatest ways of defrauding the government I've ever run into. No time to explain now, but it will keep me here several days. I hope to meet you later. Good luck!"

"Any instructions, Dad?" Frank asked.

The experienced detective thought for a moment. "Play your hunch—the desert giants," he advised. "One other thing," he added. "I'm going to bring my birth certificate with me, in case I find it necessary to leave the country. Here are photostats of yours for you to keep in your wallets. And here is Chet's too. I picked his up on the way out here."

The three boys took them and called their

thanks. Frank started the engine and taxied the plane into position. Then, with a full-throated roar, she streaked down the runway and rose gracefully into the sunny morning sky.

Frank held course directly for Chicago. By afternoon the boys could see below them the blue rippling waters of Lake Erie. Later, the eastern shore of Lake Michigan, with Chicago at its southern tip, came in sight. The late afternoon sun gleamed upon numerous planes all circling in the vicinity of the Chicago airport.

"Oh—oh! Looks as if we're going to be stacked up here!" Frank flipped on his transmitter. "56D to tower! Request landing instructions!"

"Your position, 56D?"

"Over S.W. chimney stack."

"Tower to 56D. Hold where you are until traffic clears."

Resigned, the boys joined the other craft circling above the airport. Finally their landing instructions came. Expertly Frank brought the blue ship down and into line with his designated runway. As the wheels gently touched ground, the boys stared ahead of them in sudden horror.

From the opposite end of the runway a small Cub was racing toward them in a take-off run downwind!

Frank's mind worked desperately. "If I swerve,

The boys stared ahead of them in horror

we'll crash! If I brake her, she'll nose over! If I pull up, I might hit the other ship in mid-air! Straight ahead, then, braking slowly!"

Observers gasped as the two planes rushed toward each other. At the last instant, the Cub pulled into the air. The boys could see her wheels passing a few scant feet above their heads.

"Wow!" cried Chet, who was shaking with fright.

Not another word was said until an airline pilot, who was the first to reach the boys after the near collision, pumped Frank's hand. "Well done! That fool pulled onto your runway from nowhere. Better go over and file a violation. They'll have his license in two shakes!"

Unfortunately, nobody had noticed the Cub's registration markings. The pilot had not been cleared for take-off and could not be traced. The report was the same the next morning when Frank, Joe, and Chet winged their way southwest across the plains.

At Amarillo, Texas, they stopped to rest and refuel. From here they followed the Southern Pacific Railroad tracks west. When they picked up the silvery, snakelike course of the Colorado River, Frank turned north.

"Sharp lookout for giants, everybody!" he ordered.

Dropping to an altitude of six hundred feet, he began crisscrossing the river. Eagerly the youthful detectives searched the flat surface of the California desert and the mountainous Arizona terrain.

"Frank! There—at two o'clock! A desert giant!"

Banking, Frank circled the spot, a large flat bluff a hundred feet above the water on the Arizona side.

"Long-legged fellow, isn't he?" Chet remarked. "Say, one of his feet has been bitten off by that cliff!"

"Erosion, probably," Frank guessed. "But what do you make of that smaller fellow, and those other markings next to him?"

Alongside the big giant was a figure perhaps half as large. The outline of this second giant was dug into the ground rather than scraped into the surface like his mate, so he looked more substantial.

"That's a funny design between them," Chet observed. "Looks like a cross."

"It is—a Maltese cross, an old European design. It was the emblem of a group of Crusaders called the Knights of Malta," Frank explained.

"But I thought these pictures were made by Indians," Chet objected.

"That's right," Joe agreed. "The cross seems to prove the Indians had had some contact with Spanish explorers when this giant was made."

"This wasn't the place where Willard Grafton

disappeared, was it?" Chet asked. "You mentioned Blythe, California."

"Right. And we'll head there next."

Frank went on to the California side of the river, and in a few minutes spotted another desert giant. Near him in the gravelly ground was the figure of a mammoth dog. Some distance away was a lone giant.

"This is where Grafton's plane came down," said Frank.

"It's sure amazing," Joe remarked. "I can't wait to do some investigating."

After flying over still another group of a giant and a horse, Frank said, "Guess we'd better get to the airport."

He consulted his chart and turned toward the Riverside County Airport. Frank, after getting radio instructions, brought the plane down in a perfect landing and taxied toward the hangars.

As the boys piled out of the cabin and stretched their legs, a stern, unfriendly-looking man approached them.

He introduced himself as an official of the Federal Aviation Agency. "All right, boys. Which one is the pilot?"

Surprised, Frank handed over his pilot's license, which the man scrutinized carefully. "You're the one all right," he announced gruffly. "You'll have to come with me!"

CHAPTER III

Clue Hunting

"WHAT's the matter?" Joe asked, puzzled.

The stern-looking man did not answer. He merely motioned with his head for Frank to accompany him. At the same time he took the boy's arm.

"Unload our gear, anyway," Frank called as he turned to go. "I'll see to this."

The man led Frank to a small building and into an office. Inside, a stout, jovial-looking man sat at a little desk. He seemed to be engaged in a wrestling match with the typewriter in front of him, for he had grasped it by the roller in two big hands and was tugging first one way and then the other to move it.

"Hello, Cooper. Never could use one of these things!"

Smiling, Frank Hardy stepped forward. "Allow

me, sir." He pressed the lever that allowed the carriage to slide back and forth.

"Humph!" the man grunted. "Thanks, my boy. "Who is this?" he asked, turning to the man named Cooper.

"That young Hardy pilot. The one they're after for causing that near crash at Chicago."

The man at the desk looked at Frank sympathetically. "I'm sorry, son. This may mean your license. But we can't be too careful about air safety."

Perceiving in a flash that someone had misrepresented the incident at Chicago, Frank declared, "Sir, if you think I'm responsible for that near collision, you should get the real facts from Chicago."

"Why, that's where our information came from —by long-distance phone call!"

"But not from anyone in authority," Frank insisted. "And why wasn't the message teletyped?"

"You have a point, son. We'll get in touch with Chicago at once. I'm Eugene Smith, manager of this airport at the moment."

While Mr. Cooper, the F.A.A. representative, was communicating with Chicago in another room, Frank explained to Mr. Smith that the three boys had come to search for Willard Grafton, who had disappeared in the desert nearby.

"About three months ago now." Mr. Smith

nodded. "Made quite a stir hereabouts. Never did find him, did they?"

"No, and we believe there's somebody who doesn't want him found, either." Briefly, Frank told of the Bayport eavesdropper. "I wouldn't be surprised if the false report you received about me is part of a plan to stop or at least to hold up our investigation!"

Just then, the loud disgruntled voice of Chet Morton was heard outside the office door. "I don't care if the whole United States government is keeping him in there! I'm starving! I want to eat!"

"There's a man after my heart." Mr. Smith chuckled. He called out heartily, "Come in, boys!"

Frank, Joe, and Chet had packed their belongings in rucksacks, which were more suitable for desert life than ordinary luggage. Now Joe came in bearing the neatly packed sack with his and Frank's things. Chet Morton followed with a bulging pack of his own. First he stumbled into the door. Then he lurched against the door-frame.

"Somebody ought to repack that mule's load," commented the airport manager, his eyes twinkling. He shook hands all around.

At that moment Mr. Cooper, looking a great deal more friendly, returned. "You're in the clear," he announced to Frank. "No one in authority at Chicago made that call. Why would anybody play such a dirty trick on you?"

A confusion of voices arose as Eugene Smith satisfied Cooper's curiosity and Frank explained to Chet and Joe.

"Oh—oh!" Chet rubbed his head gingerly. "I knew we hadn't seen the last of that guy who slugged me!"

When the boys emerged from the office it was nearly eight o'clock. The cloudless sky was a luminous blue. Up on the dry mountains, visible from across the desert, the shadow-filled draws looked like dark trickles of blue-black ink spilling down from the ridges.

"What a sky!" Chet exclaimed enthusiastically. "Somehow it looks bigger than it does back home."

"It's because the atmosphere is so clear," Frank commented.

Soon a sleek cream-colored convertible drew up with Gene Smith at the wheel. "Jump in!" he called. "I'll drive you into town."

Rucksacks were stashed in the back seat, and Chet climbed in after them. Frank and Joe rode in front.

As the car headed toward Blythe, where the boys would stay, the Hardy boys were surprised by the soft, warm air currents playing about their faces. Although it was nearly sundown, there was not a hint of moisture, not a trace of dew in the air.

"I thought the desert nights would be cool," Joe remarked.

"Not in summer," Smith replied. "On a night like this you can sleep outdoors with no bedroll and not get a chill. Do you plan on sleeping in the desert?"

"Later. We'll stay in town tonight," Frank answered.

"Then here's where you want to stay," Cooper said.

The convertible turned into the driveway of an attractive new motel. The building itself was white and shaped like a horseshoe. The quivering blue water of a swimming pool danced in the open space, and now and then spray leaped into the air as someone dived.

"Let's camp here," Chet agreed, piling out of the car. "They have a swell-looking restaurant!"

The boys took a room on the second floor, located in the curved section of the horseshoe. Lugging their rucksacks, they mounted the outside staircase. Ten minutes later they were in the pool. After dressing, they enjoyed a dinner that satisfied even Chet's appetite.

The next morning Frank proposed that the boys visit the offices of the *Daily Enterprise*, Blythe's only newspaper, and read up on the Grafton story.

"According to Dad, two of a detective's best friends are the newspaper and the police," the young sleuth remarked.

Later, after the three had studied clippings in the *Enterprise*'s morgue, Joe said, "Nothing new here—only that Grafton and Wetherby landed near the giant effigy outside Ripley."

"Where's their plane now?" Chet asked.

"Let's see . . . taken to Riverside County Airport by the authorities. We'll ask Gene Smith to let us look at it later," Frank suggested.

"Now," said Joe, as they left the building, "let's try the detective's other best friend—the police."

Fenton Hardy's reputation as an investigator was known even to the small Blythe police force. The chief greeted Frank and Joe warmly, but could give little new information.

"You know as much about Grafton as we do," he admitted. "Wetherby once lived here in Blythe. But that doesn't prove anything, either."

Temporarily discouraged, the young sleuths strolled down Hobsonway, the town's main street, discussing the situation.

"Tell you what!" Joe suddenly proposed to his brother. "You be Willard Grafton, and Chet and I will be Clifford Wetherby!"

"Wha-a-t?"

"I mean, you pilot the plane, and Chet and I will be passengers. We'll make the same flight they did. We'll see the same things from the air. We'll land in the same place. Maybe then we'll learn some answers."

"Let's hope we don't disappear in the same way!" Chet muttered.

"You'll never disappear, Chet," Frank needled. "There's too much of you to hide."

The stout boy made a pass in self-defense. "What say we have lunch before we start?"

After a quick meal the boys were driven by one of the motel employees to Riverside County Airport. The sun blazed upon the white buildings and the bright-colored wing surfaces of the standing aircraft. Frank and Joe wore their comfortable wide-brimmed hats, and Chet sported a new straw sombrero he had purchased.

"Whew! Talk about heat," Chet complained. "Do you know it's 108 degrees in this sun? I just checked the airport thermometer."

"Cheer up," Joe replied. "I've read that the desert sand gets as hot as 165 degrees, and we're in for some walking!"

Chet groaned. "Why don't we go back to that nice motel and take a *siesta?* That's what the Mexicans do in this heat."

"Because of Willard Grafton," Frank reminded him. "He may be in danger."

After unlocking the plane, the boys waited for air to circulate in the cabin, which was as hot as an oven. A few minutes later the trim blue craft rose smoothly from the runway. Dipping one wing, Frank banked in a circle over the airport, then headed north for the desert giants.

The boys enjoyed the scene beneath them. The Colorado River, as blue as the sky itself, was lined with beautiful yellow-leaved tamarisk trees. On the Arizona side were the brown, rugged badlands, but the California side was a rich patchwork of growing crops. Each field was a different shade of green.

"Say, I thought this was desert country," Chet marveled.

"It was," Frank answered. "You're looking at the result of irrigation in this spot. See the little ditch lines? No better soil anywhere. All it needs is water."

Farther on, they spotted the desert effigies and Frank dropped down for a landing not far from the knoll on which they had seen the lone giant.

"Assuming this is where Grafton landed," Joe mused as they piled out of the plane, "what would he have done next?"

"He'd probably have climbed up onto that knoll to look around," Frank suggested. "Come on!"

Eagerly the young detectives scrambled to the top of the steep bank to hunt for clues.

"Let's just stand here a moment and get our bearings," Joe suggested when they had reached the top.

From where the boys stood, the area ahead of them was a dry, pebble-covered expanse and nothing more, with the exception of a small bush here and there. Not far from them, however, they noticed a wide dirt path.

"Looks as if somebody took a broom and swept a walk among the pebbles," Chet remarked.

"Believe it or not, that's one of the giant's legs," Joe said.

Frank looked thoughtful. "I'm wondering," he said, "if these knolls aren't man-made. The ancient Indians could have built them and then drawn the effigies on top."

"You may be right, Frank," Joe replied. "It's a good theory. And the position of the giant may have meant something."

The boys tramped around the knoll, gazing in every direction. "Look," said Joe, desperately seeking a clue, "if Grafton stood here, what would have caught his attention?"

Suddenly Frank, who stood near the left hand of the giant, gazing down at the desert, cried out, "There's something glinting out there!"

"What is it—a mineral?" Joe asked.

"Let's find out!" Frank urged, starting down the embankment.

Joe and Chet, following close behind, saw Frank reach the desert floor, then suddenly skid to a halt and leap backward.

"Look out!" he shouted warningly.

CHAPTER IV

A Warning

A HUGE angry lizard, nearly two feet long, had raised its head and was advancing slowly toward Frank. The reptile's forked purple tongue darted menacingly from its mouth.

Frank danced back out of reach and waved his companions to a halt. "Nearly stepped on it," he said, as the lizard, hissing sharply, came on. The thick, dark-purplish body was blotched with bright yellow and covered with warts.

"Wow!" Chet's eyes popped. "What is it—a baby crocodile?"

"Gila monster," returned Frank, still watching the lizard closely. "Stay back. They're slow as turtles in a race, but I wouldn't get near those fangs. Their bite is poisonous." At this news Chet jumped backward an extra yard.

Finally the monster stopped its advance and stood regarding the boys out of cold, ugly eyes.

"Trying to scare us." Joe chuckled.

"He's succeeding," declared Chet. "Let's get out of here!"

Frank and Joe looked at each other, their eyes twinkling.

"Chet," Frank said, "you go back. Joe and I will find out what that glittering thing is."

Nervously the chunky boy considered the expanse of desert between him and the blue airplane. No telling how many Gila monsters he might meet!

"Alone?" he asked blankly.

"Sure. Go on. Wait for us at the plane."

Wistfully, Chet considered the distance again. "No," he protested in a forced hearty voice, "your folks would never forgive me if I let you down."

The Gila monster disappeared under a bush and the three boys started forward again. Ahead of them the unknown object flashed in the sunlight. After walking for some time, they did not appear to be much closer. All three boys were wearing moccasins, and the heat from the broiling sand made their feet uncomfortably warm.

"Say, do you think that thing is moving away from us?" Chet complained. He took out a gaudy handkerchief and began to mop his face.

"It's tied to the tail of a Gila monster!" Joe teased, and Frank added, "Out here you can see twenty miles instead of two or three miles as we can at home."

As the boys finally approached the mysterious glittering object, they saw that it was a twelve-inch, round, metallic rock which caught and reflected the sun's rays.

Joe rushed forward to investigate. He found the big rock studded with lovely solid-colored stones. Some were dark red, others a rich brown, a few deep green. Nature had placed these stones in the rock like jewels.

"That's beautiful, Joe," said Frank, as he came up. "What is it? Some kind of quartz?"

Back in Bayport, Joe Hardy had an extensive collection of rocks and stones. Now he carefully examined their find.

"Jasper, I'd say. Very fine specimens, too."

As slow-moving Chet joined them, he said, "Say, that stuff looks valuable. Are they precious stones?"

"Well, they're not exactly diamonds." Joe laughed. "But they *are* valuable, and no mistake."

After a quick search the boys concluded that there were no similar rocks nearby.

"That's strange. Where did this one come from? It doesn't look as if it belonged here," Joe mused.

Meanwhile, Frank had been examining the ground nearby. "You know," he announced, "this rock might have had something to do with Grafton's disappearance."

"How?" Chet asked.

"There may be other valuable stones containing jasper around here. Maybe Grafton and Wetherby spotted some from the air and landed to pick them up."

Chet nodded. "After they had gathered them, some thugs stole the stones and got rid of Grafton and Wetherby." The boy looked around him uneasily.

"That could be," Joe agreed. "But somehow I don't think so. However, they may be prisoners."

"Well, fellows, this sun isn't growing any cooler while we stand here. I vote we head back to the plane and take this rock along with us," Frank suggested.

He hoisted the big stone to his shoulder, and the three started back. Now it was their blue plane that appeared to be much closer than it really was. Again they walked for some time without seeming to make progress.

"I'll take a turn," Joe offered.

The heavy burden was shifted to his shoulder, and they went on. Finally, his face wet with perspiration, he called, "Your turn, Chet. Get a soft spot ready on your shoulder!"

With sighs and groans, the valuable rock was transferred to the beefy shoulder of Chet Morton.

"Why did we bring this old thing!" he grumbled. "How do we know it's valuable?" he demanded two minutes later.

For answer, Joe simply winked at his brother.

"This stone weighs twelve tons," protested the burdened boy. "Isn't my turn up yet? It's driving me into the ground!" Chet declared a dozen steps later.

Suppressing their laughter, Frank and Joe walked behind. Suddenly, at a signal, they sang out together:

"Gila monster!"

"Where? Where? Oh—I see him!" The stone, in spite of its great weight, was sent flying forward through the air, and Chet Morton, showing great agility for a boy his size, went sprinting in the opposite direction.

The Hardy brothers enjoyed their joke so thoroughly that for a moment they did not notice anything else. The heavy stone, however, had suddenly disappeared. "Hey! What happened to the rock?" Joe cried out.

"Guess it went in that hole," Frank said.

"Serves you both right!" Chet called. "You and your Gila monsters!"

"Why, Chet, you mean you didn't see any monster? Then why did you run?" Joe teased.

"Well . . . I guess I made a little mistake," mumbled their friend.

"You sure did. You let that valuable stone roll into a hole. To make up for it, you're elected to get the stone out."

Chet was agreeable but soon found he could not do it alone as the hole was narrow and deep.

Perspiring and breathing heavily, he begged for help. Laughing, the resourceful Hardys took off their belts and improvised a cradle in which to drag the rock back to the surface. From there, Frank and Joe took turns carrying it to the plane.

By the time the plane had landed at Riverside County Airport, it was after five o'clock.

"Just about suppertime," noted Chet with satisfaction. "A swim and a steak—"

Gene Smith came out on the field to meet them. "Hello, boys! What luck?" he called.

Chet told him about the Gila monster. Smith grinned and said, "I once made a pet out of one of those critters. Used to drink milk out of a saucer, and jump in my lap like a house cat."

"Really?" Chet gulped.

"Sure," Smith went on, with a straight face. "I taught that Gila to whistle. But it could only whistle one tune. I got tired of 'Dixie,' so I got rid of him."

The boys laughed, then showed him the jasper-studded rock. "This is all we discovered."

"Um, lucky find. We call that stuff Chinese jade. It's picked up now and then."

"Do you think Grafton and Wetherby could have been after other pieces, lost their way, and perhaps injured themselves in the mountains?" Joe asked.

Smith shrugged. "Could be. But it's a long walk."

"We have a favor to ask," put in Frank. "Willard Grafton's ship is here. May we check it for clues?"

"Help yourself. She's at the back of the far hangar over there. When you're through I'll run you into town."

"Thanks." Frank covered the jasper stone and locked the plane. The boys hurried over to Grafton's craft, a handsome red-and-white ship, with seats for four in the cabin. One of the cabin doors hung open.

"Funny they don't keep it locked," Joe remarked.

While Frank checked the instrument panel and Chet looked in the baggage area, Joe opened a little compartment similar to the glove compartment in an automobile. A penciled note on a scrap of yellow paper was all he found.

"Here's something!" Joe cried, waving the note.

Frank and Chet crowded near him to read over Joe's shoulder:

TAKE WARNING HARDYS. ROSES ARE RED.
VIOLETS ARE BLUE. WE FIXED GRAFTON.
WE'LL FIX YOU. GET OUT WHILE THE
GETTING IS GOOD.

CHAPTER V

The Mob Scene

"WHEW!" Chet whistled. "A warning! I knew this was coming!"

The Hardys' faces showed a combination of anger and perplexity. Who had written the note? Someone with a sardonic sense of humor, certainly.

"Let's not say anything about this," Frank suggested. "But we should report that the plane door was open. I'm sure the person who delivered the note is responsible."

"Yes. The hangar is out of the way," Joe agreed. "He might have sneaked in here any time, especially during the night. He knew we'd go over Grafton's plane sooner or later."

"This proves that our movements are being watched a lot more closely than we realized," said Frank soberly, pocketing the note. "I think it's time to check with Dad. Let's go!"

The boys learned that Grafton's plane had indeed been broken into and would be more carefully guarded in the future. Back in their motel room, Frank put through a long-distance call to Bayport.

"Hello, Mother! . . . Yes, we're all right. . . . Everything's fine. We're enjoying ourselves very much. . . . Can you put Dad on, please? . . . Oh!"

Covering the mouthpiece with one hand, Frank told his companions, "Dad's case has taken him out of town and Mother doesn't know where to reach him. He left us a message.

"Go ahead, Mother," Frank resumed. For the benefit of Joe and Chet, he repeated the note as Mrs. Hardy read it to him.

"Hold up work at Blythe. . . . Proceed to Los Angeles. . . . Investigate Grafton's business and interview his family. . . . Hope to see you before long. Dad."

The next morning as the three boys loaded their rucksacks, Frank grinningly whispered some order, then they went to the motel office.

"Leaving so soon, boys?" the manager inquired.

"Yes, the country doesn't agree with our friend's appetite," Joe replied.

"No place like home," Chet Morton added.

"If we've left anything behind, will you send it to our address in Bayport?" Frank asked.

"Certainly. Sorry you don't like it here."

It was not until the three friends had taken off from the county airport that the subject came up again. Then, with a grin, Joe said, "Did we look dissatisfied enough? I was trying to play my part, but I almost burst out laughing instead."

"I think that manager will remember us all right when somebody asks him about us." Frank chuckled.

"He'll say we were in a mighty big hurry to leave Blythe and go back East," Chet joined in the joking.

"Which is just what we want," Frank declared. "Meanwhile, we'll be in Los Angeles digging up clues!"

The flight was a brief one. Soon Frank, Joe, and Chet were installed in a spacious room in one of the city's older downtown hotels. While the brothers unpacked, Chet fussily inspected their quarters.

"Good solid metal fire escape," he announced, glancing out one of the windows.

Chet announced he was going on an errand and went out. An hour later, as Frank and Joe were discussing a plan of action, he returned.

"No more detective work for old Chet today," he announced brightly. "Here we are in Los Angeles, the movie capital of the world. I don't know about you fellows, but I'm going out to a lot and watch them make movies. Behold!"

With a flourish he produced three passes to a

motion-picture lot. "I called up an uncle who lives here in town," he explained. "What about it, fellows?"

"You go ahead, Chet," Frank suggested. "Joe and I will see what we can find out about Grafton and Wetherby at police headquarters, and show the warning note. Meet you back here later."

At headquarters the Hardys spoke to the detective sergeant who had been assigned to the case. "We're really stumped on this Grafton disappearance," the man admitted ruefully. "Nothing to go on. And we don't know much about Wetherby except what the Blythe police could give us."

"Do you think Mrs. Grafton would see us?" Frank inquired.

"Oh, yes. Poor woman, she'll be grateful for your interest. You might stop at Grafton's electronics plant, too. A manager operates it now."

When the detective had finished, Frank revealed what the boys had learned so far, and produced the threatening note.

"You're on to something, all right," agreed the sergeant. "Keep me posted. And call on us any time, day or night, if you're in danger!"

The brothers thanked the sergeant and went back to their hotel. Chet Morton had not returned, but the two movie-lot passes were still on the table. Joe slipped them into his pocket.

"Why not go and meet him?" he suggested. "I

wouldn't mind seeing a movie in the making my-self!"

"Okay," Frank agreed. "We can call on Mrs. Grafton this afternoon."

The movie studio was fairly easy to find. Inside, an attendant checked the brothers' passes and directed them to the proper set, where a picture about Mexico was being filmed. However, they couldn't see the bulky figure of Chet Morton among the other spectators.

In the middle of the set itself a great many people were milling around. Most of the men wore tall, wide Mexican hats. Some were in faded blue jeans with blue denim jackets, while others had on gaily embroidered outfits with silver buckles and beautifully tooled leather belts and boots. All the women wore bright-colored costumes.

"Getting ready for a mob scene," Frank remarked.

Suddenly Joe, whose eyes had been roving over the set, noticed two actors talking earnestly together in a corner. As the two parted, Joe was astonished to see that one was Chet, who was wearing his brand-new sombrero.

"Hi!" the stout boy called out as he spotted the Hardys. He hurried over.

"Who's your friend, Chet?" Joe inquired. By now the man had disappeared in the crowd of actors.

"Oh—just one of the 'extras,' " Chet explained. "He has a walk-on part in all of the mob scenes. When he saw my sombrero he said maybe I could get a job as an 'extra' too. But I can't," the disappointed Chet admitted sadly. "I asked the director. What a thrill it would have been, too!"

"Let's go, then."

After the three left the lot they passed a bank on the street near the studio. Chet called a halt. "I want to go in here a minute, fellows. That poor actor you saw with me can't leave work before the banks close, so I cashed a check for him."

"Say, you want to be careful whose personal checks you accept," Joe observed.

"Oh, this one's okay. It's a United States government check for fifty dollars. It had been made over to Al Van Buskirk—that actor I was talking to—and he endorsed it to me," Chet reassured him, and went into the bank.

A few minutes later the door opened again, but instead of Chet, a uniformed bank guard confronted Frank and Joe!

"Friends of Chester Morton inside?" he asked them gruffly.

When they said yes, the guard asked them to come into the bank. He said Chet was in trouble.

"You're my witnesses, fellows," Chet burst out in a worried voice. "Tell the cashier you know me and I'm honest."

Briefly, Joe corroborated this statement. The cashier and guard appeared satisfied.

"But what about my money?" Chet wailed. "That check cleaned me out of cash."

"I'm afraid you're out of luck," the cashier said. "We'll turn the counterfeit check over to the Treasury Department, of course."

"Counterfeit!" Frank exclaimed.

"That's right," the cashier said. "A mighty good one, too."

Frank and Joe looked at each other and instantly thought of their father's case. By any chance could Chet's counterfeit check have anything to do with it?

"Say, Joe," his brother whispered, "I think we ought to go back at once and check on that actor."

"Right."

Chet was more than willing. "That guy can't do this to me! Just let me get my hands on him!"

The three boys raced up the street. They dashed past the astounded attendant, who tried to demand their passes. They pounded along the studio pathways, straight into the set and the crowd of extras dressed like Mexicans.

"I want my money back!" Chet bellowed.

Women in the crowd shrieked. Two men were sent sprawling by the sudden charge. Cries of surprise and anger arose from all directions. Someone began to fire blank cartridges. The shrieks redoubled. Whistles blew. Orders were barked.

On one side an excited little man wearing a blue beret jumped up and down and shouted "Cut! Cut! Cut!" at the top of his lungs.

Meanwhile, Chet was rolling on the ground, wrestling with a big actor who had objected to being run into so hard. When the two had been disentangled, and order had been restored, the small wiry man in the blue beret approached the boys with eyes blazing.

"My gosh—the director!" Chet moaned. "Now we're in for it!"

The little man stepped up briskly and looked Chet up and down. "Mag—nificent!" he exclaimed unexpectedly, clapping the astounded Chet on both shoulders. "Remarkable! The very thing we wanted! Mob violence! Disorder! Wild confusion!"

"You mean . . . you're not mad at me?" Chet faltered.

"Mad at you? No!" The director snapped his fingers enthusiastically. "I'll use that scene."

"You mean you're really going to put all that in a movie? But I still want to find that actor who gave me a phony check—his name is Van Buskirk."

The director looked around the set. "He's gone. We finished the scene he was in just before you stormed the place!"

"That means I'm broke," Chet said mournfully. "I'll have to sell my infrared camera equipment."

"What are you talking about?" Joe demanded. "We need that in our work."

Frank slapped his woebegone friend on the back. "We'll stake you to the rest of the trip."

Chet grinned. "That's swell of you. But I still want my money back."

"Where does this Al Van Buskirk live?" Frank asked the director.

"I don't know. Ask at the office."

But the office did not know. The man was a wanderer, merely dropped in once in a while, and was paid cash for each job. Disappointed, the young sleuths went out and headed for a restaurant. After a hearty meal, Chet set off to visit his aunt and uncle, while Frank and Joe took a taxi to Willard Grafton's home.

Mrs. Grafton received them graciously. She was an attractive woman, somewhat younger than their own mother, but her husband's disappearance had added lines of sorrow and anxiety to her face.

A brown-haired, freckle-faced boy of about nine came in and eyed the Hardys uneasily. A younger brother, about seven, trailed him a moment later.

"Steve and Mark miss their father very much," Mrs. Grafton explained as she introduced them to the Hardys. "I'm bewildered myself," she confided to Frank and Joe when her sons had left the room. "If you only knew how grateful the three of us would be, if you could find my husband—or even discover what happened to him!"

"We'll do our best," the brothers promised.

They learned nothing new from her, except that Willard Grafton had taken no extra clothes with him, which seemed to prove he had no intention of being gone long.

Frank and Joe left the house and proceeded to the new, modern industrial building where Grafton's company still manufactured electronic self-starting devices. The boys climbed to the second floor, where they located a door bearing Grafton's name. They knocked.

A blond secretary opened it about three inches and asked suspiciously through the crack, "Who is it? What do you want?"

"Excuse me," Frank began, "we want to ask some questions about Mr. Grafton."

Before Frank could finish, the heavy door slammed in the boys' faces.

CHAPTER VI

New Evidence

"Miss—oh, miss!" Frank called through the door. He had caught a glimpse of the secretary's face. It was tense and frightened. Frank sensed that something was wrong. "You must let us in. We've come from Mrs. Grafton!"

Behind the door, the secretary seemed to hesitate. "How can I be sure of that?"

"Call her on the phone. Mention Frank and Joe Hardy!"

For about five minutes the boys waited in the hall. At last the door opened. The secretary, an intelligent, pretty young woman, seemed calm now. Before speaking, however, she locked the door. No one else was there and a tiny sign on her desk gave the girl's name as Miss Everett.

"I should have known by looking at you boys that you're all right," she apologized. "But those other men who were here this morning asking about Mr. Grafton gave me such a fright I don't trust anybody. I'm afraid to leave the door unlocked!"

"What other men? Not the police!" Joe broke in.

"Oh, no. Two big, rough-looking men. They weren't dressed very well and they talked—you know—like thugs. I wouldn't have let them in, except they said they were hunting for Mr. Grafton, so I thought they might be private detectives."

"Hunting for Mr. Grafton?" The Hardy boys exchanged looks of surprise.

"Yes. Then, as soon as they were in, they got rough and made me show them Mr. Grafton's letters and records!" The pretty girl pointed to bruises on her wrists as evidence.

"They wouldn't have acted tough if they were on the up-and-up," Joe said indignantly. "Did you call the police?"

Miss Everett shook her head. "The men said they'd make me sorry if I breathed a word about them to anybody!"

"It must be the same gang that's been bothering us," Joe deduced.

"Maybe," his brother returned thoughtfully. "But why are these two looking for Grafton if, as we suspect, they may be holding him? Could *another* gang be trying to get him away from the ones who have him?"

Miss Everett went white. "How terrible!"

"You'll have to help us," Joe appealed to the secretary. "Just tell us about Mr. Grafton. What kind of man was he? Did you like him?"

The girl knitted her brows. "Well," she began, "when I first came to work for Mr. Grafton, about a year ago, I thought he was a wonderful man. He was so dynamic, and he was making a great success of his business. People liked him because he was so gay and lively. He made friends with everyone he met. Then, all of a sudden, he changed."

"How do you mean?"

"He got moody. He would sit here brooding. When people came on business he snapped at them, and treated his customers as though they were trying to swindle him. He became suspicious of everybody."

"He must have had some reason," Joe suggested.

"Oh, yes. You see, his spirits had been very high, because he and an old college friend had pooled their resources and were negotiating to buy a new plant and double this business. Then the friend went off to Europe with all the money! Mr. Grafton didn't want to worry his family, so he never told them.

"After the trouble with his friend the only person he seemed to like was Mr. Wetherby. He said Mr. Wetherby was a challenging companion.

Then they went off together and disappeared."

"What did he mean by calling Mr. Wetherby a challenging companion?" Frank asked curiously.

"I don't know. Mr. Grafton had grown bitter and used to say that everybody in the world was dishonest, but at least Mr. Wetherby did exciting things."

"What business was Wetherby in?" Frank pursued.

The secretary shook her head. "I don't know. But I can tell you where he lived. You might find out there."

The boys wrote down the address. "Thanks, Miss Everett. As soon as we leave, you'd better call the police. They'll give you protection. Is there anything else you can tell us about Mr. Grafton?"

"Well—his only hobby was raising Shetland ponies, if that means anything."

"You never know." Frank made a note of the fact.

Back at the hotel, Frank and Joe stepped from the elevator and walked toward their room. At the far end of the hall a man wearing a short red jacket with polished brass buttons regarded them intently.

"Who's that?" asked Joe, while Frank unlocked their door.

"Just the bellman." The boys entered the room.

"Bellman, your grandmother!" Joe exclaimed as he checked a picture in his wallet. "If that isn't the guy who hid in our bushes in Bayport and slugged Chet, I'll eat this photograph!"

Excitedly the boys rushed out and searched the corridor. The bellman had vanished.

"Let's ask at the desk," Frank suggested.

After waiting some time for the elevator, the boys went down to the hotel lobby. "We want to speak with this bellman," Joe told the clerk on duty, showing him the full-face photograph.

Studying the picture, the clerk shook his head. "This man isn't one of our employees."

"But he must be. We just met him, in uniform, near our room!"

The clerk shook his head again. "Oh, Sam!" he called to a porter who was standing nearby. "Ever see this fellow before?" He showed the photograph. "These boys just saw him upstairs in a bellman's uniform."

"Not one of ours." The porter was even more definite.

"Then he must have borrowed the uniform," Joe declared.

"Must be, sir," agreed the porter. "All our bellmen are young. This man's a good forty years old. I'll call the house detective."

Together, the detective and the boys searched the room where the bellmen changed their clothes, then checked the stairways and other possible hiding places. The mysterious suspect was not around.

Disappointed and puzzled, Joe and Frank returned to their room with the detective. "What did this man look like?" the detective asked.

Joe handed him the photograph and said, "He was not heavy, but looked strong. About five-feet-nine in height."

"Well, we'll watch for him!" the detective promised as he left.

"Joe, that bellman was here to spy on you and me," Frank said grimly as he locked the window leading to the fire escape and double-checked the lock on the hall door.

"You're right. Well, let's go to Mr. Wetherby's address and see what we can find out."

The place was a boardinghouse, run by a bright-eyed, talkative Mrs. Watson. The rather stout lady, whose hair was just turning gray, met the boys at the door. White flour showed on her hands and her apron, and the pleasant aroma of baking came from the kitchen.

"Mr. Wetherby? I should say I *do* know something about him! A very good boarder he was, too, and knew good cooking when he tasted it! But come in, come in. We can't talk on the street. I'll have a pot of tea in a jiffy!"

Frank and Joe winked at each other. The price they would have to pay for information on Wetherby would be an hour at tea with the company-loving landlady. They followed her into a neat parlor.

"Tsk-tsk! That Mr. Wetherby," the bustling woman clucked. "Twelve months I tried to fatten that man—he was such a skinny fellow. I never could understand it. He ate everything I gave him, too."

Talking all the time, Mrs. Watson brought in teapot, cups, butter, fruit preserves, paper napkins, and finally a plate of fresh hot biscuits.

"He certainly should have gained weight here." Frank laughed.

"Yes—you'd think so. But then he was a peculiar man. He used up so much energy just coming and going at all hours. His hair was thinning, too, and he wasn't what you would call an old man."

"Coming and going?" Frank pricked up his ears. "Didn't he have any regular position?"

"Goodness me, he paid his rent, if that's what you mean. Do try another one of these biscuits, both of you! And when my boarders settle promptly, you know, I don't inquire further."

"They sure are wonderful biscuits, Mrs. Watson," Joe spoke up enthusiastically. "So Mr. Wetherby was a good roomer?"

"You must have been sorry to lose him," Frank added sympathetically. "But then, he didn't leave owing you any money—except perhaps a week's room and board."

"Why, dear me, no," the woman protested.

"Mr. Wetherby doesn't owe me a penny. Six months' room and board he paid me in advance, that last week, and he hasn't been here to get a bit of value for his money!"

"These are the best biscuits I ever tasted!" Joe remarked. The hospitable lady beamed. "So Mr. Wetherby had planned a little trip?"

"I suppose so," Mrs. Watson assented. "He was often away for long stays."

Suddenly, to Frank's and Joe's complete surprise, their hostess leaned forward in her chair and gave them a sly wink! "He was always mixed up in those things, you know!"

Lowering her voice, although there was nobody to eavesdrop, the talkative lady went on confidentially, "Those Latin-American countries. You know, there is always some kind of fighting going on down there. I don't pay much attention to it."

"Yes, they often have revolutions," Frank agreed.

"Well, I used to wonder, when I cleaned Mr. Wetherby's room. He had pictures of himself in an airplane—a war airplane, it was. Then there was a picture of a lot of them wearing those big ten-gallon hats, and do you know, all the men wore pistols and belts full of bullets, including Mr. Wetherby!"

"No wonder Mr. Grafton thought Wetherby did exciting things!" Frank exclaimed.

The landlady caught the name. "Yes, and he brought that gentleman here, too," she added. Evidently she was pleased to have such surprising news to tell.

"This Mr. Grafton, he told me how Mr. Wetherby used to fight in those foreign wars. He said Mr. Wetherby did it just for the adventure. He certainly admired Mr. Wetherby."

"You don't know what country he fought in, do you, Mrs. Watson?" Frank inquired.

"Dear me, I wouldn't know one of those places from another. Let me see—you boys finish those biscuits while I look around." She bustled upstairs.

"I'm stuffed!" Joe whispered. "You eat the last biscuits, Frank, so we can keep in her good graces!"

"I can't." Frank grinned, slipped the biscuits into his paper napkin, and put them into his pocket. "For Chet!"

In a moment Mrs. Watson returned. Seeing the empty plate, she exclaimed, "Dear me, you boys have been such good company, I'm going to give you this!"

She placed a copper coin in Frank's palm. "It was on Mr. Wetherby's bureau when he first came here. I wanted it for a souvenir because it looks just like a penny, you know, and he gave it to me."

"*República de Mexico!*" Frank read eagerly.

They whirled to see two brawny men climb
into the room

"Thanks very much to—the best cook in California!"

When the Hardys returned to the hotel, they found Chet waiting for them and told their story.

"You mean Wetherby used to be a pilot for a bunch of rebels in Mexico?" he asked in disbelief.

"Right. And Mexico isn't far from Ripley. Let's have a look at the map." Joe took one of the California-Arizona–northern Mexico area from his rucksack and spread it on the floor.

"Those missing men might have taken a boat right down the Colorado River into Mexico," Frank pointed out.

"Maybe Wetherby was involved in a new revolution!" Joe added. "Or some other illegal business."

A sudden rap at the door brought the boys hastily to their feet. Before they could answer, however, it opened and a man came in. He closed the door and stood facing the boys.

"The bellman!" Joe exclaimed. The man was not in uniform.

At the same time the boys heard a window open. They whirled to see two brawny men climb into the room from the fire escape!

"Yes, I unlocked the window," the bellman told the boys in a harsh, unpleasant voice. "And now you kids start talking—or else me and Ringer and Caesar over there are going to make you!"

CHAPTER VII

An Exciting Identification

INSTINCTIVELY the three boys backed up until they felt a wall behind them.

"What do you expect us to talk about?" Frank demanded, to gain time.

"About Grafton," snarled the fake bellman. "How much do you know? Come on—talk!"

The two brawny henchmen, Ringer and Caesar, advanced menacingly from the window, while the bellman moved in from the door.

"Quarterback sneak left!" Frank called, dropping to a football player's crouch.

Catching the signal, Chet, who played center for Bayport High, lowered one shoulder and plunged forward into the advancing Ringer. At the same instant Joe unleashed a body block that sent Caesar crashing backward into a desk. Frank, meanwhile, rushed the surprised bellman and threw him to the floor.

Caught off guard, the intruders fought back viciously for a few moments. But the agility and speed of the boys more than made up for the size and strength of their attackers. Caesar was groggy from his fall, and Ringer gasped for breath.

The bellman was the first to struggle to his feet. "Clear out!" he cried to his companions, knocking Chet off Ringer. Caesar was able to free himself, and the three men fled out the door. The boys went after them, but the men rushed into a service elevator. Apparently the bellman had left the door open for a quick getaway. The door slammed and the car shot downward.

"We'd never catch 'em by racing down the stairs," Joe panted.

"No," Frank agreed. "And they'll lose themselves in the street before we can overtake them."

"They didn't get away scot free, though," Chet announced after the boys reached their room. "The man I blocked out dropped this. It may be a valuable clue."

Frank took the carefully folded paper from Chet and spread it out. "Why, this is a copy of our flight plan from Blythe to Los Angeles! One of their gang must have sneaked into the airport office and copied the original. That's how they trailed us here."

"And we thought we had fooled them into thinking we'd gone back East!" said Chet, dismayed.

Frank nodded. "They outsmarted us this time. There's no question about it, we're up against a bunch of dangerous and well-organized criminals! Let's talk to the police."

At headquarters the young sleuths reported their progress. They learned that Grafton's secretary had reported the threats against her.

"You Hardys have turned up more on this case in one afternoon than we have in three months," the detective in charge asserted with admiration. He took down Joe's description of the bellman and the two strong-arm henchmen. "How do you plan to proceed from here?"

Frank analyzed the situation briefly. "We have two working hunches. First, there's the rock we found. Grafton and Wetherby might have been after minerals or semiprecious stones when this gang caught them. The other possibility is that they slipped away in a boat, probably to Mexico, since Wetherby was keen about life below the border."

"Then our first job is to hunt for more clues in the desert around the giant," Joe reasoned. "After that, we'd better hire a boat and make the trip down the river ourselves, right from where Grafton and Wetherby would have started."

"Logical reasoning," the detective said. "I wish you luck."

As the youths left headquarters, Chet exclaimed

eagerly, "Well, if we go down the river, we'll have a chance to fish. I've heard the Colorado bass are really something."

"Good idea, Chet," Joe agreed. "If we look like fishermen, we may be able to shake this gang off our trail."

"We'll need permits to enter Mexico," Frank observed. "Best place to get them is here in Los Angeles."

They headed for the Mexican consulate, where they presented their birth certificates and were given entrance cards, then all three boys obtained fishing licenses in a sporting-goods store. Soon they were air-borne again and on their way back to Riverside County Airport. They would stop at Blythe to see about renting a boat in a couple of days.

When they landed in Blythe, a brief taxi ride brought them to the town's water front. As they strolled along the river, Chet began to dawdle.

"Aren't we forgetting something awfully important? What about meals on this trip down the river? We'll need food for a month, at least."

The stocky lad had come to a full stop in front of a large market. With evident satisfaction, he contemplated the wonderful variety of foods through the broad glass window.

"Some detectives travel on their stomachs!" Joe laughed. "All right, Chet, you buy provisions while Frank and I hire a boat."

The excellent climate made Blythe a year-round fisherman's paradise, and the Hardy brothers found numerous docks along the river. They stepped onto one, looking for a suitable boat.

A graceful red-and-white craft, with two powerful outboard motors mounted on her stern, caught Joe's eye. "Plenty of power in an emergency," he commented. "Never know when we might need it!"

"Is this boat for rent?" Frank asked the proprietor, a long-legged old-timer wearing tight-fitting dungarees.

"Reckon she is." The man, whittling a stick, hardly glanced at the boys or the boat.

"Could we keep her for as long as a month?"

"Reckon so."

"Could you let us have her in a day or two?"

"Reckon I could."

"All right," Frank concluded. "We'll get in touch with you when we're ready. Is it a deal?"

"Reckon it is."

Joe laughed. "Talkative old buzzard. Not like our friend Mrs. Watson!"

As the Hardys returned to the market, Frank and Joe were amazed to see a great heap of brown food bundles seemingly walking toward them on legs of its own! Perched on top of the pile was a familiar bright sombrero, and out of the heap of packages came a familiar voice.

"Hi!"

Then, without warning, the mountain of parcels exploded. Packages flew in every direction, and rained down upon the shoulders of Frank and Joe and other passers-by. Chet Morton, who had been invisible behind the heap except for his legs and sombrero, raced down the street crying:

"Stop, thief!"

Frank and Joe hastily rescued some of the food from the street, as their friend, some distance away, brought down his man in a flying tackle.

"Give me back my money!" they heard Chet bellow as he dragged the man to his feet.

The brothers hurried over with the parcels of food.

"It's that counterfeit-check man, Van Buskirk!" Chet told them excitedly. He held the short young man by the collar and every now and then gave him a shake.

"Say, what is this, anyway?" the man protested, recovering himself. All at once he recognized Chet. "It's you again. What do you want with me?"

"I want the money you swindled from me with that phony check!"

The man looked surprised. "What do you mean? That check was all right. It was a government check."

"Yes? You tell that to the police, Mr. Innocence," answered Chet sarcastically. "You've probably got a whole bushel of them. What are you doing here in Blythe, anyhow?"

"I have a perfect right to be here. I live in Blythe!"

"Tell that to the police, too!" retorted the angry Chet.

At Blythe police headquarters Al Van Buskirk continued to maintain his innocence.

"Yes—he lives in Blythe all right," the desk sergeant spoke up. "I've seen him around town."

"Then what was he doing in Los Angeles?" Chet wanted to know.

"Listen, it must all be a mistake." Van Buskirk answered the question himself in a worried voice. "I've been ill for a while and out of regular work. All I could find was a walk-on part in that movie. When it was finished I came back here."

The man turned to Chet. "I'm sorry if I caused you to lose your money. I was taken in myself. I sold a valuable gold watch for that check!"

"Here in Blythe?" asked the officer quickly.

"No, in Los Angeles."

"Can you remember what the check passer looked like?"

"A little taller than I am, and a few years older. A spry, wiry fellow. I remember thinking he might work in some hotel, because his pants had a stripe down the side like a uniform."

Joe, on a hunch, pulled the photograph of the phony bellman from his pocket. "Al, by any chance, was this man the bad-check passer?"

Van Buskirk gazed at the picture. "It sure looks like him. Yes, that's the man! Say, where in Pete's name did you get this?"

Joe smiled. "We've been doing a little sleuthing, that's all," he answered noncommittally.

The sergeant was amazed and asked to keep the photograph. Joe handed it over. The officer now took something from his desk drawer. "Did the check you received look anything like this one?"

Both Chet and Al Van Buskirk declared, "Same thing exactly!"

The officer nodded. "This was turned in last week by the Blythe bank. Seems to be a brand-new racket."

"Officer, may my brother and I look at that check, too?" Frank inquired abruptly, again recalling the government fraud case on which their father was working. The boys examined the check and nodded to each other, but did not mention Mr. Hardy's investigation.

"Van Buskirk's story seems to check out all right, Morton," the sergeant said.

Al turned to Chet. "I'm sorry, I've already spent your money to pay bills, but I'll give you a note for the amount and pay you as soon as I can," he offered.

"That's fair enough," Chet agreed. "After all, you were fooled, too."

As the four left the police station, the Hardys

and Chet said good-by to the actor and at Frank's suggestion headed for a hardware store to purchase digging tools to use in the desert.

"I don't feel satisfied with our examination of the desert giants," he explained. "I'd like to do a little digging out there before we start down the river. I have a hunch we may find a buried clue," he said.

"Not a body!" Chet quavered.

"I hope not," said Joe. "You mean, Frank, a cache of valuable rocks or something Grafton may have managed to hide out there before he left?"

"Right."

After the purchase, the three friends took a taxi to the airport, told Gene Smith their plan, and stowed the equipment and food in the plane.

As the monoplane soared toward the desert giant, the boys discussed the exciting new developments in the case.

Presently Frank said worriedly, "I just thought of a new angle. Suppose Grafton was attacked or kidnaped?"

"Good night!" Chet exclaimed.

"Or suppose he's mixed up in some kind of racket?" Frank went on.

"How terrible for Mrs. Grafton and her boys, and Mr. Brownlee, too!" Chet remarked.

Suddenly Joe asserted, "Grafton that kind of person? I don't believe it!"

CHAPTER VIII

A Treasure Hunt

"DEEP down, I agree with you, Joe," Frank put in. "The information we have about Grafton so far is that he's honest—even if he did become soured on things."

"That's right," Joe said. "When we crack this mystery and find him, I believe he'll turn out to be okay!"

"There's our giant again," Frank announced. "Hang on! I'm going in low to scout him a little."

Frank throttled down to fly as slowly as possible while they examined the effigy. What, if anything, could it prove about buried treasure, counterfeiters, and missing men?

"I have a hunch those outstretched arms may mean something," Frank said thoughtfully.

"Why?" Chet asked.

"Because we found *our* treasure in a straight line with the left arm of that big fellow down there, unless my sense of direction has gone haywire."

Chet looked at him. "You mean the stone we found might have been a marker? But for what?"

"Wish I knew the answer," Frank said.

Joe suggested they pitch camp there for the night to see if anything happened. "Grafton and Wetherby may be in hiding around here, and show up after dark."

"I think I have the answer!" Chet broke in. "Maybe there was a stowaway in their plane. He forced Grafton and Wetherby to fly out here to meet some other member of the gang!"

Frank nodded, then said, "Not much more for us to see up here. I'm going in for a landing."

The plane rolled to a stop near the knoll where the effigy was, and the boys climbed out into the dazzling sunshine.

"Whew! Hot work ahead," Chet observed.

Meanwhile, Frank was handing supplies and tools out to his brother. "We'll take the spade and the small mattock. I've put some food and water in this one rucksack."

"I'll take charge of that," Chet volunteered. "You two carry the tools."

The young sleuths locked the plane and climbed the knoll. Then they began to hike along the left arm of the giant effigy. With their wide-brimmed hats and their digging implements they looked like a party of old-time prospectors.

"Just think if we discovered gold, wouldn't that be keen?" Chet remarked.

"There are some lost mines on the Arizona side—some that date back to the days of the early Spaniards," Frank informed him.

"How does a gold mine get lost?" Chet was puzzled. "I wouldn't lose a gold mine, if I had one!"

Joe laughed. "In the first place, the old-timers used to keep the location of their mines secret, for protection. Then sometimes mines are buried by earthquakes, or more slowly by erosion."

Suddenly Joe stopped short. "Something just ahead. Give me your spade, Frank!"

He had noticed a little sunken place roughly rectangular in shape. Unlike the hard-baked ground of the desert, this dirt seemed loose, as though it had been turned over not long before.

"Somebody's been digging!"

Frank and Chet hurried to his side. "It looks as if a hole had been dug here, and then filled in again," Joe explained, starting to dig.

Frank began tossing dirt aside with a shovel, while Chet got busy with the mattock.

"No question about it," Frank remarked as they worked. "Look at this loose soil and the size of the hole. I'd say at least two people had been on the job."

"They were wasting their time," said Chet, ten minutes later. He was wringing wet. "We haven't seen anything valuable hidden here."

The Hardys had to agree. There seemed to be nothing worth digging for.

"What do you think?" Joe asked. "Could they have cleared the hole of all valuable rocks?"

"I don't think so," his brother returned. "There would be a few traces left. We haven't seen a single fragment of the kind of rock that contains semiprecious stones."

"What were they digging for, then?" Chet wanted to know. "You mentioned buried treasure."

"I still think one might have been hidden by Indians or even Spanish explorers. The desert giant was the direction marker to show the location."

"Well, whatever it was, do you suppose Grafton and Wetherby were the ones looking for it?" Chet asked.

"Could be," Joe returned. "They were here recently enough." Carefully, he examined the ground.

"Not a footprint, or even a trace of one," he reported, discouraged. "A good solid heel print would have given us something to work with."

"No." Frank nodded. "Whoever it was knew what he was doing. He brushed away the prints in Indian style, with one of these sagebrush bushes."

Chet sat down to rest. Finally Frank gave up and flopped to the desert. "Pretty hot seat!"

"Better than nothing," said Chet. "I'm pooped!"

Joe kept on for a few minutes. By this time nearly all the soft earth had been turned over. Joe was about to give up when his shovel suddenly swept a piece of cloth into the air.

"What's that?" Frank asked eagerly, jumping to his feet.

Joe picked up the dirt-covered clotn and shook it. "A man's brown handkerchief," he said.

Chet, interested now, dragged himself to Joe's side. "You think one of the diggers dropped it?"

"I'm sure of it."

"And," Frank added, "his name begins with the letter P."

Frank pointed out the initial P, of a slightly lighter color, embroidered in one corner of the handkerchief.

"Say, this is great!" Chet cried out enthusiastically. But in a moment his face fell. "This means neither Grafton nor Wetherby dropped it."

"Correct," said Frank. "But it could mean that they have some pal whose name starts with P."

"In any case," Joe added, "we'll take it along as a souvenir or as evidence."

"Let's give up this desert search until it gets cooler," Chet pleaded. "Talk about hot enough to fry an egg. Lil ole Chet will be boiled Morton pretty soon!"

The Hardys laughed. Then Frank suggested they fly to the edge of the desert where the mountains began and rest in the cool shade.

"It's just possible there are more mineral rocks in the mountains," he suggested.

"Good idea," said Joe, and Chet nodded.

The boys went back to the plane and cooled the cabin with its air conditioner before taking off. A little while later Frank set the craft down and the three sleuths, carrying cans of food, tomato juice, and the digging tools, sought the shade of the mountainside.

"This is something like it!" Chet said with a sigh of relief as he pulled out his penknife can-opener attachment.

After the meal, Chet dozed, while Frank and Joe discussed the mystery. Presently Frank, looking up the slope, said, "I see a cave opening up there. Let's have a look at it."

The cave mouth yawned about forty feet above them. Scrambling up the slope, the Hardys stood staring at the entrance.

Frank pulled a small flashlight from his pocket and said, "Think I'll go in."

As he spoke, a menacing snarl pierced the silence of the mountain. Crouched above the cave in readiness to spring down on the Hardys was a huge wildcat!

CHAPTER IX

The Dust Devil

THE big cat looked at the Hardys out of yellow eyes. Its tail flicked in anger. Powerful muscles quivered along the tawny flank.

"Run!" Frank yelled.

Whirling, he made it back down the steep hillside in half a dozen leaps. Joe followed. Grabbing the tools the brothers had left at the bottom, the boys spun around to defend themselves.

The commotion had wakened Chet who jumped to his feet with a "Good—night!" and dashed off.

But the big wildcat did not follow the boys. Apparently satisfied that its snarl had frightened her enemies away, the animal leaped down from the ledge and entered the cave.

"That's probably a female who has young ones inside the cave," Frank said. "No wonder she was so angry."

"We found out what we wanted to know, any-how," said Joe. "Nobody's been hiding in there."

The three boys trekked through the woods, keeping their eyes open for any kind of clue to the missing men. They came to a tumble-down shack and searched it thoroughly. They found nothing suspicious.

By this time Chet had had enough sleuthing for the day. To convince his chums of this, he said, "We've been out of sight of the plane more than two hours."

"It's locked," Frank said as he tramped on ahead.

Next, Chet tried the power of suggestion. "This may be a wooded area, but it's sure hot in here." He sighed. "Picture yourselves in a nice, air-conditioned drugstore right now—with a tall frosted milk shake. And then a nice, cool swim!"

Doggedly Frank and Joe pushed on. Suddenly the resourceful Chet thought of a new tactic. "Suppose somebody breaks into our plane and steals it while we waste our time in here?"

As if in answer to this suggestion, the drone of a single-engine airplane was heard in the sky above them. Frantic, the boys raced down to the edge of the forest and peered skyward.

"It's ours!" Chet cried out.

At that instant the craft disappeared, swallowed up by a cloud. When the plane reappeared in the distance, they could hardly see it.

"No—it's not ours," Frank reassured the others at last. "I don't like it, though. What's he circling us for? Could be a spy!"

He hastily pulled out a pencil and jotted down the registration number which was printed in large figures on the underside of the plane's wing.

"You win, Chet," Frank conceded. "Let's get back to our own ship—fast."

Less than half an hour of brisk hiking brought the boys back within sight of their plane. At the same time, they saw a weird and frightening sight. A huge spiral-shaped cone of sand-filled air was blowing across the desert at great speed. It was headed in their direction.

"Wh-what's that?" Chet cried out.

"A dust devil," Frank answered grimly. "And it's a devil all right—more like a young tornado. It'll turn our plane over and smash the wings! Come on! We've got to push the plane out of the way!"

The boys dropped their tools and made a wild dash out into the desert. Could they reach the spot ahead of the dust devil, and if they did, would they succeed in moving the plane to safety?

"Faster!" Joe yelled.

When the boys reached the plane, the dust devil was still a hundred yards away, but advancing rapidly. Frank and Joe grabbed the wing struts on either side of the fuselage while Chet stationed himself at the tail.

"Now! Push!" Frank cried out.

They shoved with all their strength. The combined effort started the plane rolling. It gathered momentum. When the craft was fifty feet from its starting point, the dust devil whirled by, just missing the boys and the plane!

"Whew!" Chet exclaimed, then dropped, breathless, to the ground. "What next?"

Joe, relieved, grinned. "Don't be so impatient, pal. You'll have plenty of surprises."

"I don't doubt that," his chum answered.

The boys retrieved their tools and canteens, then climbed aboard.

"I guess we'd better not leave the plane unguarded again," Frank declared.

"Suppose we go back to Blythe and get ready for our expedition downriver," Joe proposed.

They made a quick flight back to Riverside County Airport. While Joe and Chet unloaded, Frank went over to Gene Smith's office.

"Can you tell me who is flying this ship?" he inquired, producing the number of the plane that had circled above them. "It was hanging around today up near the giants."

Gene studied the paper and checked some forms on his desk. "Let's see. . . . That's a couple of scientists from the Smithsonian Institution in Washington. Taking photographs of those big drawings on the desert."

Relieved by the information, Frank rejoined

his partners. A taxi carried the boys back to the comfortable motel where they had stayed before. The surprised but happy manager greeted them.

"Couldn't stay away, I see, boys!" he declared triumphantly. "Nobody can resist this climate. Have you tried our fishing yet?"

"No." Joe laughed. "But I guess we will tomorrow."

That evening in their room Frank and Joe studied maps of the winding Colorado River, which flowed through the state of Sonora in Mexico.

"How long will it take us to reach Mexico, do you think?" Joe asked his brother.

"Hard to say," Frank returned. "The distance is only about a hundred miles. But look at this river! Islands, sand bars, and three major dams to portage around."

"Imperial Dam is the first one," Joe noted. "That's about eighty miles from Blythe. Laguna Dam is right after that, then there's Morelos Dam on the Mexican side of the border!"

"The thing that worries me," Frank said slowly, "is having all of us away from here. Dad may show up!"

"Say," Chet spoke up, "how about my staying here? I can look around for any clues and maybe use my camera. That boat trip sounds a little rough for a landlubber!"

The problem was solved.

Soon after dawn the following morning, Frank and Joe waved good-by to Chet and the taciturn old-timer from whom they had rented their boat. They also had rented fishing rods and equipment, and had laid in a supply of bait, food, and general supplies.

Joe took the tiller first. The two powerful outboards, yoked together, were managed by a single lever. Joe headed the red-and-white craft slowly out toward the channel.

At this hour of day the river was brown in color, its surface glassy smooth. The regular, muffled sound of their motors hardly disturbed the quiet that hung over the water. Now and then ripples shaped like round, expanding targets appeared as a fish gently broke the surface to feed.

Frank, seated forward in the boat, rigged one of the rods with a spinner and dropped the line over the side. Joe saw the flashing lure, catching light from the sky, disappear astern as his brother let his line run out.

Within minutes the supple rod was bending and bucking in Frank's hands. Twenty yards astern a silvery fish leaped into the air, twitching madly, and then dropped below the surface again.

"Bass," commented Joe softly. "Play him easy."

Soon Frank brought the exhausted fish, which had broken water five more times, to the side of the boat, where Joe netted it.

"Four pounds, anyway," declared Joe appreciatively. "He'll do for lunch!"

Once out in the channel, Joe opened the throttle. The prow of the boat rose as it sped forward. The boys rounded some islands and passed under the Blythe highway bridge.

All morning Frank and Joe scanned the shore on both sides for any possible clues to the missing men or the boys' enemies. They noted the high bluffs across from Ripley, where they knew two of the giant effigies lay. The familiar area yielded no new lead from this fresh vantage point.

Shortly before noon the boys put in to shore. Frank made a small, hot fire and cooked the big bass for their lunch.

"We ought to be near Imperial Dam," Joe remarked. "We've been on the water over five hours."

A short run after lunch brought them to the wide, calm water above Imperial Dam. They put into a dock on the California side, where they were met by a big friendly man wearing a red polo shirt and a blue baseball cap.

"Howdy, boys. Going on down the river? I've got a truck waiting here. Be glad to carry you down below the dam!"

"Swell," Frank agreed. "But first we'd like some information. We're looking for a number of men wanted by the police."

As the young sleuth had hoped, his announcement brought forward several people—fishermen, boat-dock proprietors, and truckers.

"Wanted by the police? What did they look like?" the first trucker asked.

One by one, Frank gave careful descriptions of Grafton, Wetherby, the man who had posed as a bellman, and the two rough-speaking, strong-arm men.

"Waal," drawled one old fisherman, "I been coming here every day for twelve years, and I never seen any of them."

"The first two would probably be together— one is very skinny." Joe tried to prod their memories. "And the big men are called Ringer and Caesar."

The circle of men shook their heads.

"Nope."

" 'Fraid not."

"Me neither."

Discouraged, Frank and Joe helped the friendly trucker to load their boat and secure it onto a rack. After the craft was launched again below the dam, Frank paid the man, and the boys pushed off once more.

This time Frank took the tiller, and Joe looked keenly about him from the front of the boat. Abruptly, as the craft headed down the middle of the river, Joe jumped to his feet and pointed excitedly to the Arizona shore.

"Look!" he cried. "The bellman!"

CHAPTER X

The River Chase

IMMEDIATELY Frank gunned his motors, and the red-and-white craft sprang forward in the water. But the sudden, powerful roar had aroused the suspect's attention. Catching sight of the boat racing toward him, he slipped from view behind some rocks.

By the time the young detectives reached the spot, the man had disappeared completely. All they discovered was a small green motorboat moored to a pole that had been driven into the river bottom.

"Think it's his?" Frank asked, perplexed. "Maybe we'd better land and go after him. He couldn't be far away yet!"

Tall, irregular cliffs rose within a few yards of the water's edge in this wild spot. The shore was strewn with huge boulders that had broken away from the cliffs at some time in the past.

Joe shook his head. "We'd never find him in this maze of rocks. He probably knows his way around, too. Let's sit it out here. He'll have to come for the boat sooner or later."

"Unless," Frank pointed out, "he gets somebody else to come. And it could be the boat isn't his."

"Let's take the chance. I know it was the bellman. I had a good look at his face."

Already their boat had begun to drift. Carefully Frank maneuvered it back upstream. When they were in position just out in the river from the abandoned motorboat, Frank and Joe each slipped an anchor overboard.

"Out here, we can keep our eyes on those cliffs," Frank noted.

"Good idea," his brother approved. "Funny we haven't seen the bellman climbing up somewhere!"

"There's probably a trail leading to the top that's invisible to us from here," Frank replied. "Watch out for anybody spying from above!"

For about an hour the vigilant youths watched both rocks and cliffs carefully. Finally Joe Hardy decided to relax. "May as well enjoy ourselves," he said.

From their fishing box he took a bright-colored plug, which he attached to one of the casting rods. "Here goes for another big bass!"

Joe flipped the plug into likely spots along the shore. No unwary fish followed the wiggling lure back to the boat.

His brother laughed. "Too fancy. Let me show you how it's done." Digging into the bait pail, Frank came up with a long, lively night crawler. "Now, Joe, you use the artificial lure and I'll try this fellow. We'll see who gets a bass first."

"Okay, Isaak Walton!" Joe accepted the challenge.

But the fish did not seem to find the night crawler any more attractive than the fancy plug. Now it was Joe's turn to laugh.

"Just like detective work," he commented. "Sometimes you wait hours for a bite."

At that moment, out of the corner of his eye, Frank caught sight of the white shirt and blue dungarees of a man stepping from behind the rocks on shore. He told his brother, adding in a low voice, "Keep right on fishing."

Next time Joe made a cast in the man's direction. Though he seemed only to be watching his plug, he was really looking the newcomer over. "Not the bellman," he said in an undertone.

The strange man did not seem to be interested in Frank and Joe, either. He removed his shoes, waded out to the moored boat, climbed in, and untied the painter. Drifting slowly, he wound up the starting cord and gave a quick pull. Then, with his small motor put-putting, the man steered down the river.

Meanwhile, Frank and Joe had reeled in their lines and hauled in their anchors. "He may be planning to pick up the bellman," Joe whispered. "Let's keep him in sight."

With their powerful twin outboards, there was no danger of the man's outrunning them. Frank kept between fifty and a hundred yards behind the other boat.

After a while the stranger, glancing behind him, slackened his speed. Frank slowed up, too. In a minute the man cut his motor altogether. Turning, he waved the boys forward with his arm.

"No, thanks!" Instead of passing, Frank cut his motor, too.

"Wise guys!" the man shouted angrily, menacing with his fist. "Looking for trouble, are you?"

"We just want to talk to the passenger you're going to pick up," Frank replied calmly.

"I ain't goin' to pick up no passenger. So get on your way!"

"Is that so?" Frank returned. "I think we'll hang around, anyway, and make sure."

Furious, the man took the starting cord and whipped his motor into life again. Calmly, Frank did the same.

"How far will he go?" Joe wondered.

The man chugged on steadily without taking notice of the Hardys again until both boats entered the wide expanse of water above Laguna Dam.

In the middle of the reservoir, the surly stranger cut his motor again. When he saw that Frank did the same, he turned on the boys in a rage.

"I'll yell for the cops!"

"Don't bother," Joe broke in. "Here comes a police launch now!"

Frank turned and caught sight of the big police cruiser traveling swiftly across the water in their direction. As the launch bore down on them he heard the boat of the bad-tempered stranger pick up speed. Frank turned quickly. The suspicious motorboat was racing toward the Arizona shore. Even as the police came alongside, they saw the man leap from the boat, dash up the beach, and disappear.

Then Frank and Joe noticed that one of the policemen had been watching the strange man through binoculars. "It's that stolen motorboat, all right!" he announced to his fellow officer.

"He beat it when he saw us coming," the second policeman answered.

"Did you say that boat was stolen, Officer?" Frank called out.

"Right. We've been looking for it all day."

"We have reason to believe the thief is prob-

ably a member of a gang wanted by the police,"
Frank said.

Briefly and clearly Frank and Joe related their
discoveries in the Grafton case to the two startled officers. "And we're sure this motorboat was
going to pick up the fake bellman!" Joe finished.

The officer in charge sized up the situation
quickly. "This looks like serious business. You
boys had better proceed downriver according to
your plan. We'll start a search here for this boat
thief and your phony bellman. They couldn't
have gone far. When you get to Yuma, check in at
police headquarters for news."

In another moment the police launch was roar-

ing toward the Arizona shore, while Frank and Joe steered for the boat docks on the California side.

Again Frank questioned the group of fishermen, loungers, and truckers on shore about Grafton and Wetherby and the three known members of the gang, but without success. Then Joe added a description of the surly boat thief, but nobody recognized him, either.

"Well, if they've been here, they sure kept out of sight," observed Joe, after the boys had launched their boat again below the dam.

"Don't be too sure," his brother cautioned. "They may have been here. These people could

even have seen them. The trouble is, they don't remember. Most people don't fully develop their powers of observation. After all, they're not detectives!"

"That's true," agreed Joe, who had taken over the tiller once more. "Say," he added suddenly, "have you noticed how dark it's getting? I can hardly make out the ripples that mark the snags and sand bars."

The blurred forms of birds dipped and swooped over the water in search of insects. Only when they were silhouetted against the pale, luminous sky could the boys see them clearly. Bats flew about, veering sharply with their awkward, fluttering wings.

"Time to pitch camp," said Frank. "We were up early, and we've had a long day sleuthing."

Gently, Joe ran the nose of the boat up to a sand bar that made a pleasant beach. Frank leaped out carrying an anchor, and Joe followed with the rucksack containing food and cooking utensils.

The boys kindled a cheerful fire with bits of white, dry driftwood. Soon the pleasant sound of sizzling pork chops and their sharp, appetizing aroma filled the air. Joe, the cook, squatted on his haunches before the fire, turning the chops in the fry pan, toasting and buttering bread, and putting on water for their coffee. Meanwhile, Frank opened a can of applesauce and another of vegetables.

Tired from their long day, the young detectives leaned comfortably against a driftwood log and ate their supper from tin plates. Firelight flickered on their faces and threw shadows over the surrounding rocks.

"Now for dessert," said Joe happily, skewering a marshmallow to toast over the dying fire.

Later, as Frank spread out their sleeping bags, he remarked, "We'll be glad to be inside these bags toward morning. It'll be damp right next to the water."

Before turning in, Joe Hardy baited a strong line, attached it to a stout stick, and cast it into the river. "Night is a good time for catfish!" he said. "Let's see what we have in the morning!"

The boys crawled into their bags and slept soundly on the soft sand. Early the next morning they breakfasted upon the big catfish that Joe had hauled in on his night line.

"Tastes pretty good, for such an ugly customer!" Frank marveled.

Two hours later the boys docked their motorboat at Yuma, Arizona. A short walk from the river brought them to police headquarters.

"So you're the Hardy brothers!" the desk sergeant greeted them. "No news on your boat thief and his accomplice up at Laguna Dam, I'm sorry to say. Looks as if they've slipped through our fingers."

Disappointed, Frank and Joe returned to their boat and headed down the river once more.

"Anyhow, we know they've been using the river," Joe figured. "The only thing to do is stick to our plan. Maybe we'll run into Grafton or Wetherby or some others involved in this mystery."

"I hope they let us through!" Joe said as they neared San Luis on the Mexican side.

"Why shouldn't they?" returned his brother. "We aren't smugglers!"

A uniformed customs official came to meet them. *"Buenos días,"* the *aduana* inspector said. "You would like to visit our country? Have you some proof of identity with you? Visitors' permits, perhaps?"

"We sure do." Frank and Joe handed over their permits.

When the *aduanero* saw the names on the cards, he frowned, bobbed his head up and down, and said stiffly, "Sorry, but you will not be allowed to come into Mexico!"

CHAPTER XI

Stranded

"BUT why not?" Joe cried in amazement. "You have our visitors' permits!"

"That will not be enough," the inspector snapped coldly. "How do I know who you are? Two young men in a large hurry to get over the border. It must be for some secret purpose—perhaps illegal—or you would wait for *mañana*. You may be using the names Frank and Joe Hardy. It fits perfectly. We have been warned to expect you."

"There must be some mistake," Joe insisted.

In a flash Frank caught on. For the second time their enemies were trying to delay the young detectives by deliberately misleading the authorities!

"I can prove to you, Inspector," he said, "that we're on the level—that our names really *are* Frank and Joe Hardy."

Frank took out his birth certificate and suggested that Joe get his.

"Here's proof," Frank said.

Startled, the inspector took the photostats that the boys held out. Doubtful, he frowned, read them, turned them over and over, and peered at their official seals.

"I cannot find anything wrong with these," he admitted reluctantly.

"Of course not," Frank said. "We're not the ones trying to hide anything. We're hunting for a missing man. We think he may be the victim of a gang of vicious criminals—probably the same ones who warned you about us. Who were they?"

The inspector gazed at the young sleuths for several seconds. Then apparently satisfied that they were honest, he said, "Two big, rough-looking fellows. Talked pretty tough. They told me they were private detectives. Showed me their credentials, too. Do you know them?"

"Ringer and Caesar!" Joe exclaimed to his brother. He turned back to the inspector. "Those men probably are members of the gang we're trying to find. They may have buddies in your country. If you don't believe our story, call the police at Yuma. They'll back us up."

"I will," the man agreed. "The chief of police there is a friend of mine."

He placed the call and a few moments later said, "Carl? . . . This is your friend Sanchos.

Something funny is happening here. . . ." Looking at Frank and Joe, he described them and gave their story.

Even from where they stood, the boys could hear the crackling voice on the other end of the wire. When the chief stopped talking, the inspector turned to them with a relieved look on his face.

"He says you are okay," Sanchos told them. "The chief asked me to tell you the bellman has not been caught. Who is this bellman?"

Frank told him what little he knew.

"So sorry for all this trouble," the inspector said. "Please to continue your journey."

Frank and Joe grinned. "No hard feelings. But what about those two men? Which way were they crossing the border?" Joe asked.

"They were going to the United States."

"Hm." Frank considered, then said, "We'd better go on into Mexico, Joe." His brother nodded, knowing that Frank meant they should continue their hunt for Grafton.

Under the fierce afternoon sun, the boys sent their boat on into the state of Sonora.

"I have a hunch," said Joe, "that we're getting hotter on the trail of this mystery."

"One thing is certain—that gang didn't want us in Mexico," his brother returned. "There must be something down here they're trying to hide!"

"Do you suppose it's Grafton?"

"Could be. But there must be something else, too. I think Grafton is only part of it. Why does this gang want him in their game? And does their racket have something to do with those counterfeit United States government checks?"

"I'm convinced that if we can find Grafton, we'll find that out, too," Joe declared.

In this area the river was shallow and difficult to navigate. Frank did the steering while Joe kept a sharp lookout on the river and along the shore. for any suspicious persons.

Suddenly, as they rounded a bend in the twisting river, the motors suddenly quit.

"Oh, no!" Joe moaned. "This *can't* happen!"

"Just did, though," his brother muttered, bending over the engines. "Let's see. Fuel okay."

Joe scrambled to the stern to help. The boys tried everything they could think of to start the motors, but the big, new outboards remained silent. Meanwhile, the boat was drifting downstream.

"Too complicated for me," Joe had to admit.

"Let's get out of this current, anyway," Frank advised. Skillfully he steered the powerless craft toward a sandy area on the right bank. They beached the boat and the boys bent industriously over the engines again.

"We have company," Joe announced after a few minutes.

Jerking his head up, Frank caught sight of a

child's face with sparkling eyes and gleaming white teeth, peeping at him mischievously from behind a clump of bushes along the bank. Then it ducked down, and the boys heard a loud giggle.

Instantly a whole chorus of giggles arose. Another face popped up for a peek, and then another. But when the Hardys looked, all disappeared again.

"Scared of us." Frank laughed, rummaging in the rucksack. "Here's something to bring them out."

Standing in the open so that he could be seen clearly, Frank began to peel the wrapper from a big bar of chocolate. The curious faces started to reappear, flashing shy smiles. Frank offered a piece to one bold, black-haired little fellow, his face bronzed by the sun. When the boy accepted, the others came out of hiding.

"They're Mexican Indian children," Frank stated.

He and Joe, using their high school Spanish and pointing, explained their trouble. The little black-haired boy nodded knowingly and signaled for everyone to follow him.

Off in a line they started, the six little children and then the Hardy brothers. Half a mile's walk brought them to a small adobe farmhouse almost hidden by a field of high, green corn.

Like a swarm of bees, all buzzing excitedly, the children plunged into the corn. A moment later they were back, bringing with them a grave-looking Indian with a hoe in his hand.

As Joe excused himself to look around, Frank explained their trouble as simply as he could. "Our boat will not run. Is there a mechanic somewhere near here?"

The Indian had nodded after the first sentence to show that he understood. In answer to the question, he shook his head and made a sweeping gesture with his arm, as if inviting the boys to look. On one side was rough, somewhat hilly country; on the other, desert, completely wild except for the little farmhouse and the small field near it.

"Nearest mechanic in Riita," the farmer said.

"Riita—a long walk?"

The Indian nodded. Frank's hopes fell. But he took the opportunity to describe Grafton and Wetherby as clearly as he could to find out if they had been seen. But the Indian again shook his head. No Americans had stopped at the farmhouse for more than a year.

At that moment a wild whoop split the air. "Yippee! Frank! We're saved—here—around the house—come look!" Joe Hardy dashed out suddenly from behind the house, beckoned wildly, and dashed back again. "It's beautiful!" Frank heard him exclaim with admiration.

Closely followed by the Indian, Frank strode quickly around the little farmhouse. Joe Hardy was seated at the wheel of an ancient automobile almost as high as the house itself.

The car had a broad, flat roof, with blue sky showing through the holes in it. The glass of the big square windows had been knocked out long ago. The whole car was rusty except the wooden wheels. But the narrow tires were filled with air!

"I think I have the gearshift figured out, Frank!" Joe called down excitedly. "See if we can rent it!"

"This . . . automobile . . . does it still run?"

"*Si. Si!*" The Indian nodded vigorously and patted the ancient radiator with affection.

"You will rent it to us, so that we may drive to Riita for a mechanic?"

The Indian looked with approval at Joe Hardy, who seemed to be delighted with the old relic, and nodded.

The native drew them a map of the roads they would follow to reach Riita. Then he took off his hat and his faded denim jacket and bent over in front of the radiator. From the front seat, Frank and Joe could see his muscles straining.

"What's he doing?" asked Frank.

"Cranking. No starters in these crates, you know!"

With a grating, metallic sound the old engine turned over. Joe worked the unfamiliar levers and pedals furiously. Suddenly the whole car seemed to explode in a series of backfires like pistol shots. It stood there banging and vibrating as though threatening to shake into a thousand pieces.

"She runs!" Joe gloated.

The Indian, who had disappeared, now rushed back with a jug in each hand. He was grinning.

"What's that for?" Frank wanted to know.

Because the car was making too much noise for him to be heard, the man simply tapped the radiator cap significantly. Joe took the jugs and nodded. "In case she boils over!"

Frank handed the man some American money and climbed aboard.

"*Adiós!*" the boys shouted above the din.

The Indian and his children waved good-by.

Bucking suddenly in low gear, the ancient vehicle clattered onto the rutted track leading from the farm. Soon the boys were bumping along at a good rate of speed.

"On to Riita!" Joe shouted in high spirits.

"You hope!" retorted his brother, hanging on to his seat.

They had gone about three miles when the road suddenly began to climb a hill, ascending in a series of hairpin turns. Halfway up, the engine started to wheeze and sputter. Joe shifted to a lower gear. Gallantly the vehicle ground forward. On the next turn Joe shifted down again. Still the tired motor strained and threatened to stall.

"We haven't any lower gear!" cried Frank. "We'll never make it!"

"Oh, yes, we will—I have an idea!"

Maneuvering carefully, Joe managed to turn the car completely around, so that they were heading downhill.

"Where are you going now?" cried his brother. "Riita!"

Joe threw the car into reverse gear, and the old automobile began to grind steadily up the hill backward! "According to the old-timers, reverse is the best gear in these old crates!" he shouted to his brother above the noise.

When they reached the top of the ridge, Joe turned the car around again, and they started their descent.

"Oh—oh, I should have used a lower gear," Joe said worriedly as the old jalopy picked up speed.

"Brake her a little," Frank advised.

"What do you think I'm doing? The brake pedal is on the floor now and the emergency won't work!"

Completely without brakes, the old car plunged madly down the mountain road, careening wildly around the turns and going faster and faster every second.

CHAPTER XII

The Escaping Stranger

"HANG on!" Joe shouted as he hugged the hill-side. "If we meet another car on the turns, we're done for!" Frantically he squeezed the rubber bulb of the horn, and as the cumbersome vehicle plunged wildly downhill, the old-fashioned horn blared out:

"Ska-goog—ah! Ska-goog—ah! Ska-goog—ah!"

Joe took the turns like a race driver, crowding to the inside as he went into them. He knew that any sudden twist of the wheel could cause the high automobile to turn over. Luckily there were no hairpin turns on this side of the ridge.

At last they were down off the hill, shooting forward over the level ground.

"Boy!" Joe exclaimed. "I wish this bus had a speedometer. We're practically flying!"

"Never mind," his brother answered in relief. "After that drive, you're qualified for the 500-mile race at Indianapolis!"

"Well, we'd better come to a gas station soon," Joe called back over the noise of the engine.

"Yes, to get these brakes looked after."

"Brakes. Who needs brakes? What we need now is gasoline." With one finger Joe indicated the car's fuel gauge.

"Empty!" Frank exclaimed.

Anxiously the boys scanned the road ahead of them. Though they could see for miles, there was no sign of a house—let alone a gas station—in any direction.

"Wait a minute," Joe noted suddenly. "What's that crossing the desert in front of us? Looks like a line of telegraph poles."

The poles stuck up at regular intervals among the big cactus and other desert growth.

"If they're telegraph poles, there's probably a railroad alongside them," Frank reasoned.

At that moment the car's engine began to cough and sputter. The whole vehicle bucked as the motor stopped, started again, then quit entirely.

"There goes the last drop." Throwing the gearshift into neutral, Joe announced, "We'll coast just as far as we can."

When the ancient wheels finally rolled to a stop, the car was barely a hundred yards from the tracks. With the last bit of momentum, Joe had pulled his vehicle to the side of the road.

"Stuck in the middle of nowhere," Joe complained as the boys piled out. "Stranded again. First the boat and now this car."

"Cheer up!" Frank said encouragingly. "This railroad goes someplace where there's a mechanic. There's bound to be a train or a station. Let's start walking."

"Which way? Toward the good old U.S.A.?"

"No. Riita."

Quickly Frank checked his watch and then noted the position of the sun. "It's just six o'clock now. At this time of year the sun would be slightly north of west. I'd say this way—southeast."

Walking on the crossties and crushed stone, the brothers set out at a good steady pace.

"Boy, I sure wish a train would stop for us," Joe remarked wearily.

After a walk of about an hour, Frank's keen eyes picked out a small building beside the tracks. "Now we're coming to something," he said, encouraged.

"Yes," Joe agreed, when they were closer. "Looks like a little station. And say! There's a truck, and some fellows loading things. If we hurry, maybe we can catch a ride to some town and find a mechanic to fix our boat."

"Sh!" Frank commanded. "Are they yelling to us, or what?"

As the boys stood still, shouts and loud, angry words in Spanish reached them.

"They're stealing the freight!" the agent shouted

"If those aren't shouts for help, I don't know my Spanish!" exclaimed Frank. "Let's move!"

Breaking into a fast run, the boys swiftly covered the distance to the little adobe station.

The first thing they saw was a man trussed up and rolling on the ground. He was shouting as loud as he could:

"Help! Thieves! They're stealing the freight!"

At that moment two men emerged from the station door, carrying a heavy box. Grunting, they moved with their load toward the waiting truck.

"Now!" Frank shouted, breaking into a sprint. "While their hands are full!"

Frank's well-aimed punch knocked one to the ground, stunning him. Joe had leaped on the other man. As all four went down together, the heavy box fell on the leg of Joe's man, causing him to cry out in pain. Seizing the advantage, Joe gripped his sturdy opponent around the middle with his legs and began to pommel him. But the strongly built man twisted away. Grabbing Joe by the shoulders, he flung the boy off, jumped up, and ran for the truck.

Meanwhile, Frank had plowed again into his adversary. While the man lay on the ground, winded, Frank dashed over to the freight agent.

Now, as the truck's engine roared into life, the thief suddenly leaped up and made a break for the vehicle. Joe was too late to stop him. In a moment the truck was speeding across the desert away from the station.

"How is the agent?" Joe asked, returning to his brother.

"Very well, thanks to you," the man replied in excellent English. "As soon as I have rubbed some life into my wrists, which are very sore from the rope, I will shake your hand in gratitude."

Seeing the surprised expressions on the faces of the Hardy brothers, he explained, "My name is Leon Armijo. I went to school in the United States while my father was working there."

"Who were those men, Leon?" Frank asked.

"Freight thieves. Men like that often try to rob lonely stations. They took me by surprise. Except for you two, they would have everything. As it is, they got nothing. Where did you come from, so luckily for me?"

"From a car that broke down." Joe laughed in answer. "That is, if you can call it a car."

"We were on our way to Riita," Frank explained. "It's urgent that we get a mechanic as quickly as possible to fix a boat we have on the river."

"Nothing is easier." Leon Armijo said. "I will have the next train stop for you. But that is too little return for your help. Where is your car? I shall have it fixed. When you return here, it will be waiting for you!"

Frank Hardy grew thoughtful for a moment.

"Good. The trouble is, we may not come back this way for some time. We're looking for a mechanic to repair our boat, and it may be easier to get back to the river another way. But, you see, we rented the car from a farmer and he may need it."

"Do not worry," said their new friend. "I myself will return the car."

"In that case we accept your offer with thanks." Frank told the agent where the Indian lived.

"It's nothing," Armijo went on. "The next train is a freight north to Mexicali. But the one after that is a coach bound south to Riita."

While they waited for the train, the grateful agent shared his supper with the two hungry boys. Then all three went outside. The sun was just setting far across the desert.

"This is just a shot in the dark, Leon," Joe said, "but have you seen any Americans around here—any Americans at all—for the past few months?"

For a moment the Mexican was silent as he searched his memory. "I do not know whether this will help you," he said doubtfully, "but I will tell you a little story. This is a very lonely station. Very few Americans come here. But several weeks ago, about this time of night, a strange man arrived on foot. A freight train was stopped here. I was unloading packages when I noticed this man sneaking around the cars."

"A tramp looking for a free ride," Joe suggested.

"So I thought," Leon agreed, "and I went over to chase him away. He was too tired to run from me. When I reached him, he said he was from the United States. He pleaded with me to let him climb into one of the empty freight cars. Somebody was pursuing him, he said."

"Was he a fugitive from the police?"

The agent shrugged his shoulders. "That was what I did not know. He had walked a long way across the desert. I felt sorry for him. Just then I saw the lights of a car approaching the station very fast on the desert road. This man thought it must be his pursuers. Well, the train was about to leave. I had to decide quickly. I helped him into an empty boxcar.

"Soon afterward—when the train had gone—the car arrived. Two men, I think from your country, hurried into the station seeking the tramp. They said he was a criminal. Somehow, I did not believe them, and pretended I knew nothing and did not understand. They went away."

"Why didn't you believe them?" Frank questioned.

"Well, because this man—this tramp—he did not seem like a criminal. He was an educated man. He spoke very well. Although he was frightened and in trouble, he complimented me for my English. I trusted him."

"How about the other two?" Joe asked.

The Mexican frowned. "When I lived in the United States I saw that kind of man sometimes. Big, rough men who speak badly. Bullies. Men who have no respect for other people, or for law and order, either."

Excitedly, Joe burst out, "Frank! That tramp may have been Grafton. What a break!"

"I think so, too," his brother agreed. "We know that Grafton was well educated, pleasant, and people liked him. It all ties in. And the other two sound like some of the toughs we tangled with in Los Angeles."

"Listen, Leon," Joe persisted. "Was this tramp tall or short? Was he frail or well built?"

"A tall man," replied the agent promptly. "Thin, wiry. He had walked a long way and was very tired, but not exhausted."

"That checks." Frank nodded.

"One thing more, Leon," Joe pursued. "Which way was that freight train heading?"

"North—toward the border."

"Hmm," Frank put in thoughtfully. "In that case, why hasn't Grafton returned home by now?"

"Maybe he didn't make it," Joe suggested. "That gang might have caught him again. Maybe he was afraid they were watching his home. Or maybe he stayed in Mexico to try and rescue Wetherby!"

"That's an idea," his brother agreed. "I'd forgotten about Wetherby. How come he didn't escape with Grafton?"

At that moment Frank, Joe, and Leon Armijo heard the whistle of an approaching train. "Here is the freight to Mexicali," the agent announced.

"Mexicali—and then the border!" Joe exclaimed. "That's the train for us. If Grafton went north by freight, we will, too!"

"But what about your boat?" Leon Armijo asked.

"It will have to wait," Joe replied. "A good thing for us it broke down!"

Hastily, Leon gave them directions. "I will flag the train. When it has stopped, you two sneak down the track and climb into a car."

"Right—and thanks for everything, Leon!"

The three shook hands. Then the agent went out with his flag, and the Hardys slipped off in the dark to make a circle back to the track.

Soon the train rumbled in and stopped. Armijo carried some packages out and handed them to a man in a car just behind the engine. The train started again, with a long chain of jolts all the way to the caboose as each car got moving.

Although the engineer did not know it, when he left the lonely desert station he was carrying two new passengers in one of his boxcars.

CHAPTER XIII

Spanish Hardys

CROSS-LEGGED, the brothers sat before the huge open doorway of the boxcar and looked out. Under the pale, white light of the moon, the desert passed steadily before their eyes with its rocks and mesas, its scrubby plant life, an occasional wild animal, and the isolated adobe houses which showed no lights at this late hour.

"What do we do next?" Joe asked.

"Stick with the train as far as we can," Frank proposed. "That's probably what Grafton did. Let's see what happens."

"In the meantime, I'm going to sleep," Joe announced, curling up. "I don't care how bumpy this car is!"

"Good idea," Frank seconded in a sleepy voice.

Tired from the hair-raising automobile ride, the long walk, and then the violent fight, the two boys fell into a deep sleep.

Crash! Bang! Crash!

Opening their eyes with a start, Frank and Joe found the bright light of morning flooding the boxcar. Next they discovered two strange men banging the side of the car with heavy sticks.

"Wake up, tourists!" one ordered in a cheerful voice. "You will not go to the United States today. A taxi awaits you—a special taxi."

"The Mexican police," Frank muttered, blinking, as he recognized the uniforms.

"Yes, my friend," went on the good-humored voice. "The border police. Last stop in Mexico. All free riders get off here."

"Are we in Mexicali, then?" Frank inquired.

"Yes—in Mexicali. Now, come along. The other tourists are waiting."

Frank and Joe followed the officer past the motionless boxcars toward the front of the train. There a number of Mexicans, most of them dressed in the faded denim suits of farm laborers, were clambering into the back of a truck.

"Who are all those guys?" Joe asked sleepily.

"Free riders—like us," his brother answered. "Trying to get over the border illegally."

By now the boys had reached the truck. The occupants extended friendly hands to help them aboard.

"Where are they taking us?" Joe inquired.

"Jail, probably."

"Jail!" Joe echoed. "They can't put us in jail!"

Suddenly the cheerful guard, who had been boosting Joe from behind, stopped and looked into their faces attentively, then walked to the side of the road.

"What's he up to?" Joe wondered.

"Search me—reporting to his chief, I guess."

From the truck they could see the man talking to the officer who seemed to be in charge. Then in another minute they were rattling through the streets of Mexicali.

At the police station the boys leaped to the pavement. Immediately the guard, who had preceded the truck in a jeep, pulled them to one side, while the other prisoners filed into the station.

"Get on your way—fast!" he whispered. "Jump into the cab of the truck."

The vehicle's engine was still running, and no sooner had Frank and Joe climbed in and slammed the door than the driver headed out of town.

"What's up?" asked Frank, bewildered.

"The police are looking for some smugglers," the driver answered. "Your name is Hardy? The guard was instructed to release you and send you away. I heard the order. I don't know what it's all about."

"That's funny—" Joe began. But suddenly the young detectives looked at each other. "Hardy—it must be Dad!" Frank exclaimed.

"Do you mean Dad got us out of that scrape? Then he must be around here somewhere. He may be working on this Grafton mystery himself!"

Thoughtfully Frank shook his head. "I doubt it. If he were, why would he want us out of the way? His other case may have brought him to Mexico."

"And we landed right in the middle of it!" finished Joe. "So what now?"

"Keep on looking for Grafton," his brother replied. "Dad's all right, I'm sure." Turning to the driver, the youth asked, "Where are you taking us?"

"Algodones."

"Then we'll be back on the river and can have our boat fixed."

"You are detectives—working with the police?" the man asked.

"We're searching for an American who disappeared in Mexico," Frank answered.

"Go to the hotel on the main street and wait," the driver advised. "I will have the police repair your boat and bring it to Algodones."

An hour later the brothers were purchasing some much-needed clothes in a small drygoods store in Algodones. Both bought sturdy dungaree trousers and short dungaree jackets to match. Frank added a bright bandanna, and each boy got a pair of the handsome high-heeled, hand-tooled, Mexican leather boots.

Later, as they were about to register at the town's main hotel, Frank had an idea. He not only spoke in Spanish, but he translated his name, when signing the guest book, as "Francisco Fuerte."

Quick-witted Joe Hardy signed as "José Fuerte."

"Good Spanish names." The clerk smiled his approval.

"Yes." Frank laughed. "May I look at your guest book, please? I wonder if two of our friends passed this way?"

"Were your friends fishermen?" the clerk asked.

"Well—not exactly," Joe replied. "They were making the trip downriver by boat. They're older than we are—men about forty years of age. Both are thin, but one is taller than the other and more athletic looking. Maybe he stopped here on his way back. Grafton is his name."

The attentive clerk shook his head. Meanwhile, Frank had checked the book without results and now stood plunged in thought.

"Our friends may have stopped some place along the way," he suggested to the clerk. "One of them is a lover of Shetland ponies. He could never pass a Shetland pony ranch, if he found one, without stopping there."

"Then perhaps he never came this far," the smiling clerk remarked. "There's a pony ranch just over the border—between Yuma, Arizona, and Andrade, California. The Miller Ranch."

"Thanks." Frank laughed. "Maybe we'll have to pry him loose from there!"

Alone in their room, Joe complimented his brother. "Nice work. That ranch may be a real lead. And if anybody snoops in that guest book, he won't find the name Hardy—in English, at least."

After a hearty supper, the boys decided to telephone Chet. While Joe kept watch for possible eavesdroppers, Frank called Blythe from the restaurant's telephone booth.

"Thought I should be hearing from you fellows," boomed the hefty boy's cheerful voice. "What's up?"

"We're on Grafton's trail," Frank reported.

"Say, that's great! What can I do?"

"Just tell me one thing—have you seen Dad, or heard from him?"

"No. Everything's quiet here. But say," Chet went on enthusiastically, "you should see the nighttime pictures of the desert I'm getting!"

"Don't tell me you go out on the desert by yourself at night!" Frank teased.

"I have a swell new friend who goes with me," Chet admitted. "A private airplane pilot named Jim Weston. He's interested in infrared photography too."

"Well, try to be at the motel at this time every

night," Frank urged. "We'll call you if we need anything."

"Roger!" their friend agreed. "Hope you find Grafton!"

All the following morning Frank and Joe drifted in and out of stores, gas stations, and restaurants, talking casually to people who might have seen Grafton or Wetherby. The boys had no luck and went to sit in the hotel lobby. Just after noon the truck driver who had brought them from Mexicali walked in.

"Your boat is at the dock," he greeted the Hardys. "The repairs have been made. It runs perfectly."

"Hot diggety!" Joe exclaimed. "What are we waiting for?"

Francisco and José Fuerte checked out of the hotel. Sporting their blue-dungaree suits and handsome new boots, the boys followed the driver to the water front. The familiar red-and-white boat was waiting for them, with their rucksack and other equipment on the front seat.

"It was a very small matter," replied the policeman at the wheel, when Frank tried to pay him for the repair. "Do not trouble yourself. We are always glad to help our neighbors to the north."

"We sure are grateful." Joe smiled.

In a few minutes the young detectives were out on the river once more, heading upstream under the warm afternoon sun. Soon they had crossed the border again—this time without any trouble.

When the docks of Yuma, Arizona, became visible on the right, Frank headed across the river toward the California shore and they docked their boat at a public wharf.

"Now for that pony ranch," he proposed. "Shouldn't be more than a mile or two from the river."

Joe hoisted the rucksack to his shoulders and followed his brother from the dock. Together they set off along a faint trail over the desert.

"This leads straight to the ranch, according to the boat-dock owner," Frank noted.

After trudging for some distance, the low buildings and the corrals of the ranch came into view.

"There she is," Frank called.

"Just in time, too," Joe replied, as he swung down his pack. "These new boots are killing me. Hold up a minute while I slip into my moccasins again."

Quickly Joe pulled out the comfortable shoes and dropped them before him on the ground. Then, hopping on one foot, he pulled off the handsome but tight-fitting right boot and slipped his stockinged foot into one of the moccasins.

"Ouch!" he shouted, quickly pulling his foot out again. Holding it in both hands, he hopped around on the other leg. "Ow—boy!"

"What's the matter?" Frank asked, laughing.

"It isn't funny. Feels as if I'd stepped on a fishhook, only worse!"

Wondering, Frank peered into the small, light-weight shoe. Suddenly he began to stamp on the moccasin viciously with the heavy heel of his own boot.

"Fishhook, nothing!" he cried out. "There was a little yellow scorpion in your shoe. He must have stung you!"

Both boys looked carefully at the small, straw-colored insect that Frank shook out of the moccasin. It had a long curving tail with a deadly barb at the end.

"That's what he got you with," said Frank. "They hide in dark places during the day. He must have crawled into the rucksack down in Mexico. Sit still now. There isn't a moment to lose!"

Carefully Frank examined the sting. Working rapidly, he bound his new bandanna around Joe's leg. Then, using a pencil, he completed the tourniquet and tightened the pressure on his brother's leg.

"That will slow the flow of blood, so the poison can't circulate," he observed. "Now let's get to that ranch!"

Fortunately, two cowboys saw the Hardys, one leaning heavily on the other, approaching the ranch. They sped out in a jeep and introduced themselves as Slim Martin and Curly Jones. After hearing what had happened, they took the Hardys quickly to the ranch house, where Joe was put to bed by the owner, Mr. Miller.

"Get me ice cubes—quick!" Mr. Miller ordered. He was a short, capable-looking man, whose face was bronzed by the weather.

Bags of ice were applied to the wound, and the owner gave Joe a shot of an antidote to counteract the scorpion's poison.

"Lucky we were able to treat you so quickly," the rancher remarked after it seemed that the danger was past. "That sting could have killed you, or at least made you mighty sick. Where were you fellows heading?"

"Here," Frank replied. Briefly, he described Grafton. The owner and his foreman Hank, who had come in, looked at each other.

"Why—that sounds just like Bill Gray," the foreman remarked.

"Bill Gray—Willard Grafton . . . hmm . . . might have changed his name just a little," the owner agreed.

"You mean he's here?" Frank and Joe cried together excitedly.

"Whoa!" said the owner, chuckling. "This man, Bill Gray, worked for me a couple of weeks. Sounds like the person you're after. Too bad, but I don't know where he went."

CHAPTER XIV

Exchanging Names

ALTHOUGH excited by the news that Grafton might have worked at the ranch, Frank Hardy was determined to make sure.

"This Bill Gray—can you describe him, Mr. Miller?"

"Guess so," the ranch owner responded. "Let's see. . . . He was tall, all right, kind of thin but pretty well put together. Hadn't shaved for days and looked like a drifter. I wasn't going to give him a job, but I was glad to take him on after I saw the way he worked with the ponies."

"How was that?" Frank asked.

"Easy," Mr. Miller recalled with approval. "Gentle. Knew just how to handle 'em. I don't mean he just knew horses, either. Horses are a little different. This man knew his Shetland ponies."

"That's Grafton!" Joe sang out from the bed.

"And was he alone?" Frank went on, somewhat puzzled. "Nobody with him? Nobody came to see him?"

Mr. Miller shook his head. "A nicer, more likable man you couldn't find. Quiet, though—didn't talk about himself. I was sorry to lose him. Wouldn't say where he was going, either. But"—the rancher's chair scraped as he got up suddenly—"I have something that may be a clue. Gray left it in the bunkhouse. I'll get it." Mr. Miller and the ranch foreman left the room.

Instantly Joe said, "Frank, maybe Grafton broke off with Wetherby for some reason and is still heading north!"

Frank nodded. "Grafton won't talk about himself, and uses an assumed name. He could have become involved in a shady deal and is trying to get away from somebody. But who?"

"Maybe," Joe suggested, "he has enemies who haven't been able to find him, but they knew we're trying to, so they're following us, hoping we'll lead them to Grafton!"

"Well, if that's true," Frank said thoughtfully, "Grafton hasn't been out of their hands very long. Otherwise, those hoodlums wouldn't have attacked us in Los Angeles. They would've followed us."

"All right. Let's turn the tables," Joe proposed eagerly. "We'll set a trap."

At that moment Mr. Miller returned, waving

an ordinary postal card. "Here we are," he called. "Doesn't make much sense, though."

Carefully Frank examined the smudged writing on both sides of the card. Then he handed it to his brother.

"Hmm—postmarked Denver, Colorado," noted the young sleuth. "Addressed to Bill Gray."

"Yes, but read the salutation," Frank urged in excitement.

"Let's see." Joe squinted at the blurred scrawl. "It says 'Dear Willard.' This clinches it, Frank!"

"It's the man you're after, eh?" asked Mr. Miller. "What do you make of the rest of it, then?"

The entire message consisted of three letters, scrawled across the card in a heavy dark pencil and blurred by handling.

"Y—E—S," Joe spelled, frowning. "Yes."

"Yes—what?" the curious rancher wondered.

"I think I can answer that question, Mr. Miller," said Frank suddenly. "But first, tell me, did you like Gray, or Grafton? Would you be willing to help him?"

"Best man with a Shetland pony I ever saw," the rancher repeated emphatically.

Frank smiled. "Grafton's *not* a cowboy, Mr. Miller. He's an industrialist from Los Angeles. Not long ago he disappeared. We think he may have been kidnaped but escaped.

"For some reason, he hasn't gone to the police but is trying to hide from his kidnapers. I believe we can find him, but the abductors are trailing us. Will you help us trap them?"

"I sure will!" Miller answered.

"Good. My brother has a plan."

"Here it is, then," Joe began as the others gave him their attention. "Slim and Curly have given me an idea. They're young and they look a lot like Frank and me. Suppose we lend them our new outfits, and then after supper let them go to Yuma in our boat."

"Any spies will think they're us," put in Frank. "Go on, Joe."

"Meanwhile, we'll go to Yuma by car dressed like a couple of cowboys from the ranch. If we time it right, your men should arrive about dusk —too dark for anyone to tell who they really are. We'll be hiding nearby. Then, if we see anybody following the cowboys, we'll nab them!"

"First rate," Frank approved. "What do you say, Mr. Miller?"

The rancher was a step ahead of them. Already he had gone to the door and called to his wife, "Edith, ask Curly and Slim to step in here!"

After thanking the two cowboys who had rushed him to the ranch, Joe explained his plan.

"I'm game," said Curly Jones, who resembled Frank. "Bill Gray was a good *hombre*."

"Count me in," Slim Martin added. "Sounds like fun."

When the two cowboys had gone out again, Mr.

Miller turned to Frank. "We'll give you an early supper, and then you can go in to Yuma and get set." He grinned. "But before you receive one mouthful to eat, you must explain to me what that postal card means!"

"Fair enough," Frank answered, laughing. "Put yourself in Grafton's place, Mr. Miller. He escapes out of Mexico with no money, nobody to go to for help, and perhaps kidnapers on his trail. He knows a lot about Shetland ponies. So he takes this job with you, to earn some money and to rest up. But then he starts worrying again—"

"Why?" the rancher questioned.

"Too close to Mexico," Joe replied. "Too easy for the gang to find him."

"Right," Frank agreed. "He wants to get farther away. So he writes to a friend in Denver, telling some of his troubles and asking for a job."

"And he tells the friend to address him as Bill Gray and just to answer yes or no!" Joe joined in excitedly.

"Right again." Frank smiled. "But the friend was careless. He wrote 'Dear Willard' on the card."

Mr. Miller gave a whistle. "I think you've figured it out! So he left for a job in Denver. But what kind of job?"

"Mr. Miller, you said he was wonderful with ponies—really expert," the young detective reminded him. "We'll find him on a Shetland pony ranch not far from Denver, I'll venture to guess!"

"I'll bet you will, at that!" the rancher exclaimed with admiration. "Now, why couldn't I figure that out myself?"

Shortly before sundown that night, two youthful figures, dressed in the Hardys' new dungaree outfits, walked from the Miller pony ranch toward the Colorado River. Slim carried a rucksack on his back. When they reached the boat dock, the two walked directly to a red-and-white motorboat powered by twin outboard engines.

"Everything as we left her, Joe?" Curly Jones asked.

"Right, Frank!" his companion answered, throwing the rucksack aboard.

"So Grafton's in a Yuma hotel," said the other. His voice carried easily to the fisherman and men loafing along shore. "Well, let's go!"

As the craft sped across the river toward the boat docks at Yuma, the young man steering her asked the other, "Well, how'd we do, Slim?"

"Pretty good, Curly. We make a good Frank and Joe Hardy!"

Two hours earlier a jeep had left the Miller ranch, throwing up a cloud of dust as it sped along the road to Yuma. At the wheel, wearing the big Stetson hat and checkered flannel shirt of the cowboy Curly, was Frank Hardy. Next to him was Joe Hardy, although from a distance he looked like the ranch hand Slim.

When the brothers reached Yuma police headquarters, they were not recognized by the desk
sergeant who had been cordial to them a few days
earlier. "What can I do for you fellows?" he asked
gruffly.

"Let us see the chief. Tell him Frank and Joe
Hardy are here."

Startled, the sergeant looked closer. "Well, I'll
be . . . I didn't know you boys. What's up?"

"We're going to spring a little trap, Sergeant,"
Frank answered.

A few minutes later Joe explained their plan to
the chief, who nodded in approval. "Sounds good.
I'll send Wes Benton with you. He's on our plain-
clothes squad."

Wes Benton turned out to be a tall, sturdily
built man who had a great respect for Fenton
Hardy as a detective. After briefing the man on
the case, Frank and Joe set out with him for the
water front.

The three took up a position on a bank over-
looking the Yuma boat docks. Numerous small
craft kept coming and going, churning up the
water constantly. On the dock itself were a great
many boat enthusiasts who, Benton said, went
boating in the evening.

Among them, a Mexican instantly caught
Frank's attention. He was the only person on the
dock who did not appear to be interested in some
boat or other. The man stood fairly close to the

three sleuths, and was peering across the water toward the other shore.

Just then Joe announced in a low whisper, "Here they come now."

The Hardys' red-and-white boat chugged into sight and headed straight for the dock. As the cowboys moored, Frank saw the mysterious Mexican stare at them intently. When Curly and Slim climbed the bank toward the street, the man followed.

Without a word, Frank pointed out the suspect to his companions. Then the trio also walked up the street, keeping as far behind the man as he kept behind the two ranch hands.

As Curly and Slim entered a hotel, the Mexican ducked into an alley. From there he edged up to the hotel window and peered inside.

"That's our man, all right," said Wes Benton gruffly as he closed in.

The Mexican was so intent on his spying that he did not notice the three come up behind him. Wes Benton seized his arm in a strong grip.

"You're under arrest!"

Whirling, the man tried to run, but he found himself face to face with Frank Hardy. Joe blocked the other side, and at the same time the two cowboys burst from the hotel door. Hopelessly outnumbered, the Mexican went along quietly to the police station.

"His name is Rivera Acuna," declared the chief,

examining the man's papers. "No record of legal entry into the country. Book him as an alien, since he won't talk, and put him in a cell."

An officer led the prisoner away. Delighted with the capture, Curly and Slim shook hands with the Hardys, who thanked them for the impersonation.

"We'll be headin' back now in the jeep," said Curly. "The boss will want to hear what happened."

"Too bad you'll miss the rest," Frank replied.

"How's that?"

"I have a strong suspicion our prisoner will escape from here in a very short while. What do you say, Chief?"

The officer grinned. "Yes. And if we let him go, he'll take us right to his friends."

"To bad we'll miss it." Slim and Curly shook their heads regretfully. "But we got to go."

No sooner had the cowboys driven away than an officer hurried in to report: "He finally discovered the cell wasn't locked and sneaked out the back way."

"Let's go!" said Wes, slapping his holster.

"No shooting when we find his companions," pleaded Frank. "We want these men to talk."

Slipping into the alley, the boys saw the Mexican disappear behind the corner of a building. Stealthily but swiftly, they followed. Wes and four officers came some distance behind.

The fugitive hurried through a series of back alleys, made his way to a little shack, and slipped inside. Fearing that the man might warn his friends, Frank and Joe made a rush for the entrance themselves.

"You're all under arrest!" Frank cried out as they burst into the room.

Three startled Mexicans whirled to face the Hardys.

"Only two kids," said the man who had escaped, advancing threateningly. "Get them!"

Ducking low, the boys met the rush of the three men head on. The only lamp was smashed instantly. In the pitch-dark room a wild and furious struggle began.

CHAPTER XV

An Important Discovery

SUDDENLY the beam of a powerful spotlight cut through the darkness of the little shack. Police whistles screeched outside. The three Mexicans scrambled to their feet and bolted for the door— straight into the arms of Wes Benton and the other officers!

The prisoners were hustled into two waiting police cars, one of which was carrying the spotlight. At the police station the Mexicans, sullen and bruised from the fight in the shack, would answer no questions.

"We want to go home," Rivera Acuna repeated over and over in a dull voice.

"Nothing much we can do with them," admitted the chief, disgusted. "They're only small fry. I was hoping for bigger game."

"Still, they won't be following us any more,"

Joe reminded him. "Now Frank and I can go ahead and find Grafton. We'll go back to Blythe, pick up the plane, and fly to Denver."

Bright and early the next morning the young detectives started back up the Colorado River. After portaging around the two huge dams, they ran with the throttle of their powerful engines wide open. Even so, the hundred miles of difficult, twisting river took them all day to cover.

Around suppertime they reached Blythe. At the dock was the boat owner, whittling a stick unconcernedly.

"Reckon it was a good trip?" he asked. Carefully he folded the money Frank gave him and stuffed it into the watch pocket of his jeans.

"Reckon it was," Frank answered with a straight face.

As the Hardys set off for the motel Joe grinned. "Reckon he was whittlin' all the time we were gone."

"Some people like a quiet life." His brother laughed. "Wait'll we tell Chet about our adventures!"

Chet Morton was not to be found, however. Nor did he show up at the motel. Finally the Hardys checked with the owner. Chet had phoned in a message that he was going on an overnight trip with Jim Weston. In the morning the brothers were forced to take off for Denver without him.

Flying almost directly northeast, Frank and Joe had soon passed over the state of Arizona. In the distance the high, rugged ridges of the Rockies thrust up against the blue sky.

"We'll need altitude here," Frank declared.

Below them, they could see the Rio Grande where it was still a swift mountain river. They crossed the Continental Divide near Pike's Peak and then landed at Denver.

At the airport tourist information desk, the young sleuths obtained the name of the Redlands Shetland Pony Ranch nearby. "You can rent a car right here at the airport," they were told.

Minutes later, the boys were driving through the mountainous country outside Denver.

"I can't believe we're so close to finding Grafton," Joe said nervously. "Suppose this hunch doesn't pay off?"

"Cross that bridge when we come to it."

Soon the car entered the yard of the Redlands Ranch and stopped beside the house. As Joe got out, he caught a glimpse of a tall, slim, broad-shouldered cowboy entering a long, low building that looked like a stable.

"Guess we'd better ask here about Bill Gray," Frank said, heading for the house.

"Never mind. Follow me!" Joe called. Astonished, Frank set off at a run behind his brother.

Joe entered the stable and paused for an instant to look around him. He saw a row of square stalls, all of them empty but one. In that one the tall ranch hand had just begun to currycomb a frisky-looking black-and-white pony.

"*Sooo,* girl," crooned the man's gentle voice.

As Frank and Joe came over, the pony's big eyes rolled nervously, and she shifted about in the stall. Patiently the cowboy soothed her once more.

"Mr. Grafton?" Joe inquired tentatively.

The man's head came up with a furious jerk. "What's that?" he demanded, looking from Joe to Frank with startled, frightened eyes. "My name's Gray—Bill Gray!"

"Don't be afraid of us, Mr. Grafton," Frank said kindly. "Your uncle, Clement Brownlee, asked us to find you. He's been trying to locate you for months."

"I—I mustn't be found," the man retorted, still alarmed. "It's too dangerous for my family. Furthermore, I don't know who you are. How can I believe your story?"

"I'm Frank Hardy and this is my brother Joe. We're sons of Fenton Hardy, the private detective. We're your friends, Mr. Grafton!"

"Friends?" The harried-looking man gave a sigh. "I don't have any friends."

"What's become of your friend Clifford Wetherby?"

"My *friend* Wetherby," repeated Willard Grafton with bitter sarcasm. "The one man I still had some respect for, and he played me for an easy mark. He sold me on going to Mexico. Said we'd have some adventures."

"Wait a minute," Joe interrupted. "You mean you and Wetherby went to Mexico together?"

Grafton nodded. "Yes. By boat and at night. We managed to sneak over the border without reporting to the authorities and joined his gang."

Joe whistled. "So Wetherby is part of the gang!"

"Yes," Grafton continued. "He set a guard over me, and threatened to harm my family if I escaped and reported him. I got away, but then I lost my courage because of the warning about my family. So I just disappeared. I hopped a freight and came across the border. I sent a letter to Wetherby under the name he used in Mexico, saying I wouldn't squeal. But they're after me just the same. They think I know too much."

"Mr. Grafton, how did Wetherby talk you into the trip?" Joe asked.

"You wouldn't understand." Grafton shook his head hopelessly. "I'd just been double-crossed in business and felt very disillusioned. I wanted to get away for a while. Then Wetherby asked me to take a trip in my plane. We'd hardly started when Wetherby said he had a surprise and ordered me to land in the desert. Then he took me to a waiting boat. I thought Wetherby was a brave adventurer. It turns out he's nothing but a crook!"

"Then it's our job to bring him to justice," Frank pointed out. "Only you can help us do that. What's Wetherby's game? What racket is he in?"

The frightened man was determined to reveal nothing more. "No." He shook his head. "It wouldn't do any good."

"Look here, Mr. Grafton," Frank began in a firmer tone. "You can't hide away for the rest of your life. Too many people care about you. Everybody we've met on our search has had a good word to say about you. We visited Mrs. Grafton and your sons, too. I suppose I don't have to say how they feel about your disappearance."

At the mention of his family, the unhappy man burst out, "But what can I do? I *can't* go home now!"

"Why not?" asked both boys.

"Wetherby would kill me," Grafton wailed, "and he'd harm my family."

"Tell your story to the police," Joe urged.

Again Grafton shook his head hopelessly. "I can't go to the police because I guess I'm a criminal now myself."

"What do you mean?" Frank asked in amazement.

"Wetherby knows. I—I passed several bad checks for him."

"Checks? What kind? United States government checks?" Frank caught him up sharply.

"No. Personal ones."

With Grafton steadfastly refusing to go back to Los Angeles, Frank and Joe were in a quandary. But they elicited a promise from him that he would not run away and would think over their proposition. On the strength of this the brothers drove off to a highway restaurant where they could have supper and think the matter out. From the restaurant Frank put through a call to Chet at Blythe.

"Chet? This is Frank, in Denver, Colorado. I have news!"

"So have I!" cried the stout boy in high excitement. "I thought you'd never call. I've found a great new clue. I can't tell you now—just get here as quick as you can! What are you doing way up at Denver, anyhow?"

"We've just found Grafton, that's all."

"What? No kidding!"

"Yes, but keep it quiet. We'll be back as early as we can tomorrow."

"I'll keep my news until then," Chet said, and a moment later Frank concluded the conversation.

After supper the two young detectives drove slowly back to the Shetland pony ranch. Now that the work of the day was over, the ranch hands were enjoying themselves. Some lounged in the yard, while others played cards and told stories in the bunkhouse. Grafton sat cross-legged on his bunk, mending a saddle. He appeared calmer than he had in the afternoon.

"Looks like a nice bunch of men to work with," Frank commented as Grafton joined them outside.

"Yes," he agreed. "They're good fellows. Nobody knows anything about me here. I get along with them all."

Slowly Frank, Joe, and Grafton strolled away from the buildings toward the fields where the herd of Shetland ponies was pastured.

"I can understand why you don't want to leave here," Frank admitted. "It's a nice place, and you're safe—both from the law and from Wetherby. But we have a proposition for you, Mr. Grafton."

"What is it?" Grafton faced them squarely. Already he seemed to have regained some of his confidence.

"Don't go back to Los Angeles just yet. Help Joe and me and our dad to track down Wetherby and capture him. That will square you with the law and get rid of the threat to your family."

Grafton hesitated only a moment. Then, gratefully, he shook Frank's extended hand.

"It's a deal. Where do we go from here?"

"Back to Blythe."

Grafton looked troubled. "Wetherby has spies in that area," he objected. "They'll know me right away."

"Leave it to me," Frank assured the man. "I have an idea of how to take care of that!"

CHAPTER XVI

The Disguised Cowboy

LATER that evening, after the cowboys had retired to the bunkhouse, the kitchen of the Redlands' ranch home presented a strange scene.

On a chair in the middle of the room sat Willard Grafton. A sheet was draped about his body from the neck down. Above his head Frank Hardy brandished a pair of scissors in one hand and a comb in the other, like a barber working on a customer. With a flourish, Frank cut away a lock of Grafton's brown hair, and then stepped back to observe the effect.

"Ooops—got an ear that time," warned Mr. Redland, a boyhood friend of Grafton.

"What do you think you're doing there, barber?" Joe demanded with pretended severity. The rancher and his wife laughed heartily as Grafton winced.

"I'm adding thirty years to Mr. Grafton's age," Frank defended himself. "Who ever saw an old drifting cowboy with such well-cared-for hair? Off it comes!"

Snip! Snip! When Grafton's hair seemed ragged enough, Frank sprinkled on some powder from a special Hardy make-up kit which Joe had driven back to the plane to fetch. After a good rubbing, Grafton's rich brown hair had become a dingy gray color. "No shaving for a while now," the young barber ordered. "Tomorrow, whiskers gray, too!"

Another powder gave a dry, grizzled look to Grafton's skin. Then Frank added a few age lines with a make-up pencil. "Now, stand up."

Pulling off the sheet, Willard Grafton obeyed. His outfit consisted of down-at-the-heel boots and tattered clothing that the other ranch hands had discarded.

"That old cowpoke has sure seen better days." Mr. Redland chuckled.

"Let's see you limp across the room, Mr. Grafton," Joe directed.

Obediently the disguised man moved slowly, in a series of awkward, painful jerks, toward the wall.

"No, no—not that way," Joe objected. "A person who limps doesn't walk like that. He walks smoothly—and just as fast as we do!"

Demonstrating, the young detective hobbled

briskly across the kitchen as though he had had a
limp for years.

"Say, that's right, Joe," Mr. Redland declared.
"I've noticed myself—once a man gets used to
his limp, he moves around pretty fast."

After Grafton had practiced walking for a while,
the group prepared to break up.

"Now remember," Joe instructed Grafton,
"you're an old unshaven cowboy with a limp.
Early tomorrow you hitch a ride to the airport
with one of the hands. Then you stow away on
our plane. If anybody chases you out, come back
later and sneak on again. We'll show up about
noon."

Frank, Joe, and the disguised Grafton stayed
at the ranch house overnight and set off in the
morning.

When the Hardys boarded their plane the
next day, they discovered a seedy-looking old
codger cowering in the back seat.

"Who's that?" Frank demanded gruffly.

"A stowaway, sir," Grafton pleaded, grinning.

"Keep your head down!" Joe warned. "We're
not supposed to know you're here until it's too
late!"

The plane roared down the runway and as-
cended into the sky. In all directions its passengers
could see the jagged ridges of the Rocky Mountains. Grafton was thankful for the speed of their
flight back to Blythe.

"To think it took me three days to hitchhike that distance!" he declared.

"There's Chet, waiting with a rented car," called Joe as they taxied up to the hangars.

The door of the plane opened and Joe Hardy jumped down. Frank followed and then held the door open.

"Come on! Get down from there!" he ordered harshly.

Meekly a gaunt, disheveled old cowboy lowered himself to the ground. When the boys strode toward the car he hobbled respectfully behind.

"Who's he?" Chet demanded, bewildered. When the Hardys did not reply, he added, "Not Grafton!"

"Hush!" Joe hissed in warning, glancing around.

"This old coot stowed away on us, Chet," Frank announced in a loud, angry voice. "Keep your eye on him while we make a report, will you? I mean to have him arrested!"

Catching on, their chum responded, "Right. Get over here, you!"

Frank and Joe then walked over to Gene Smith's office, actually to find out about leaving the plane for a few days. When they returned to the car they discovered Chet alone, looking frantically in all directions.

"Where's Graf . . . that cowboy?" asked Joe.

"Gone! Vanished," wailed Chet miserably. "I

swear I just peeked inside the hood for a second, and he disappeared into thin air. And after you guys had such a job finding him. Oh, I could kick myself!"

"Never mind that," Frank cut him short. "Scatter, quick! Find him! His life may be in danger!"

"I'll take the parking lot," Chet volunteered, hustling off.

"Then I'll search the hangars," Frank said. "Joe, you check the planes and groups of people on the field itself."

Quickly Joe peered into the cabins of three light planes standing nearby. Ducking underneath the fuselage of the third, he found a small crowd of men gathered around the loading door of a two-engine cargo plane.

Laughs, jeers, and shouts of encouragement came from the men, who craned their necks to get a better look at something. Slipping through to the front, Joe saw that a wide ramp had been placed in the door of the plane, and that a beautiful coal-black horse, her head tossing from side to side, her eyes rolling, ears flattened back to show her distrust, was resisting all efforts by an airport employee to lead her down the ramp. Cowering against its mother's flank was a handsome colt of the same color.

"Easy, girl," one man coaxed.

"Take the colt first!" another shouted.

Suddenly a tall, shabbily dressed old man hobbled forward onto the ramp.

"Look out, Pop! You'll get hurt!" somebody cried.

But the old man, speaking constantly in a low, soothing voice, continued to approach the nervous mare, with one hand extended, palm up. As the horse nuzzled into the outstretched hand, the noisy crowd quieted with respectful surprise. Taking advantage of the silence, the old cow hand slipped closer, still coaxing, soothing, reassuring the animal while he gently grasped the halter. Then, turning slightly, he started down the ramp, and the horse, stepping gingerly, followed. The little colt clopped obediently after.

"Nice work, old-timer!" Joe Hardy stepped forward and clapped the old man on the back. At the same time he seized the cowboy's arm and pushed him brusquely away from the horse's grateful owner.

"Boy, you gave us a fright, Mr. Grafton!" Joe whispered tensely.

Well pleased, Grafton only answered, "Lucky I had some sugar in these pockets."

"Don't forget to limp," Joe warned as the two hurried to the car.

Both Frank and Chet had returned already. To prevent any more misadventures, the youths put Grafton in the car and got started immediately. When Chet was introduced, he told Grafton how pleased he was at his return. Then Chet was apprised of the plan to capture Wetherby and his gang before Grafton made his return known.

"And now, Chet," Frank inquired, "what's this big news of yours?"

"Just wait till you hear it!" Chet exclaimed. "Two nights ago I was out after some close-up pictures of desert animals with Jim Weston—my new friend. We got some good shots, but in one of them, without knowing it, we got a man! He was heading somewhere away from the river."

"Well, that's a little queer," Frank commented. "Not earthshaking news, though."

"You haven't heard the half of it. *This was the same guy I photographed back in Bayport!*"

"The bellman?" Frank and Joe chorused. "That *is* a clue!"

Noticing Grafton's bewilderment, Frank explained.

"We think he's a member of Wetherby's gang, since he has already spied on us and even attacked the three of us." Frank described their hotel assailants. "Do you know them, Mr. Grafton?"

"Can't say I do," the man replied. "My kidnapers were Mexicans." Then he changed the subject. "Where are we going to stay, boys? I'm not very presentable in this getup."

"At our motel," Joe replied, after a moment's thought. "Frank and I will keep the manager busy while Chet sneaks you in. You pretend just to be helping us with our gear. Even though you're disguised we don't want you to be noticed."

Joe's proposal worked without a hitch. While the Hardy brothers were in the motel office, Grafton carried their rucksack to the room as though he had been hired to do so.

Bustling about officiously, Chet ordered four steak dinners sent up to the room. "Mr. Grafton would have to eat alone if we went to the restaurant," he explained.

Although Grafton remained a little reticent, Frank and Joe were glad to see that he appeared to enjoy the boys' company.

"Now, down to business," Frank began after the meal. "I can't wait to get over on the Arizona side and do some investigating around the giant effigy there. Chet's picture of the bellman is a good lead. And the fact that we found digging near the lone giant's left hand may mean other digging by the same people in a similar location."

"Yes," Joe said, "and those people who were digging may be connected with the gang. We may even pick up the men out there."

"I suggest," Frank said, "that we rent a cabin down near Ripley and hire another boat. Then we can cross the river as often as we want to."

Willard Grafton was the first to approve. "I'm for it. Sounds good, Frank."

"Okay. We'll leave in the morning. Any other ideas?"

Chet spoke up. "Suppose you three drive out and hire the cabin. I'll buy supplies, rent a boat, and come down with my pal Jim Weston. He's trustworthy, and he'll be a real help."

"Good thought," Frank agreed. "We might rent the cabin in his name, to throw the gang off our trail."

At noon the next day Frank, Joe, and the disguised Grafton were with a farmer, inspecting a comfortable-looking water-front cabin just across from the Arizona giants. The place had a wide river-front porch from which the rocky bluffs on the other side could be seen clearly. Beautiful golden tamarisk trees grew all around the cabin.

"Nice place," remarked the farmer, who owned it. "Off by itself, though. That's the reason some folks won't rent it." He handed Frank the key and drove away.

Together, the boys and Grafton clumped onto the porch to unlock the door. The noise of their boots caused a sudden, dry rattle underneath the porch. Then came a rustling sound.

Suddenly the long body of a bright diamond-backed sidewinder twisted and slithered into the sunlight beside the porch!

CHAPTER XVII

The Chemical Fog

"DON'T move!" Frank flattened back against the door and spread both arms to restrain his companions.

But the gesture came a split second too late. Panic-stricken, Grafton had leaped from the porch—straight into the path of the swift-moving snake!

For an instant the man's long legs were exposed to the danger of a bite, since he had landed with one boot on either side of the writhing, diamond-backed body. But before the reptile could coil to strike, Grafton had dashed to safety. The snake started to slither back to the porch.

"Grab one of these—quick!" Joe had discovered a pile of wooden stakes, each about three feet long, next to the porch. Armed, the boys charged after the retreating reptile. Unable to reach cover, the sidewinder turned and coiled itself menacingly. Warily Frank extended his stick. *Bang!* The snake, nearly five feet long, crashed into the target with such force that the weapon was knocked from Frank's hands.

Seizing the opportunity while the snake lay extended on the ground, Joe rushed in and with a well-placed stroke killed the reptile.

"Wow!" Frank exclaimed. "I didn't know those babies packed such a wallop!"

"That settles him, anyhow," Joe said. "It's okay, Mr. Grafton—the snake's dead," he called to the scared man, who had watched the fight from fifty yards away.

Reassured, Grafton came back. "Thanks, fellows," he said.

"You had a mighty close call," Joe reminded him. "Why did you jump like that?"

"I—I panicked, I guess. You see, I was brought up in dry country like this. When I was a little boy, I nearly died of rattlesnake venom. Ever since, I've been terribly afraid of snakes."

"Well," Joe suggested, "let's get out of this sun, anyhow. I'm glad I don't have a thermometer. I'd hate to know how hot it is in this desert."

But Willard Grafton refused to move toward the cabin. "No, I couldn't stay there now," he declared nervously. "That snake may have a mate."

"But you can't just stand out on the desert," Joe argued. "And we can't keep you in town—it's too dangerous. After all, you're in hiding, you know!"

Not until Frank and Joe had poked and probed thoroughly under all parts of the cabin did Grafton move to enter the building. They found the big single room of the cabin pleasantly cool. Bunk beds, two-tiered, had been built against three walls. Hanging on the fourth were cooking utensils and fishing equipment for their use. The boys decided to wait for Chet and his friend on the porch, where they could watch the river.

"Wish they would hurry up," Joe remarked impatiently. "I'm getting hungry. Besides, we have work to do to crack the rest of this case."

At this new mention of the case, Frank shot an inquiring glance at Willard Grafton, who returned a little smile. "All right," he said. "I've been holding out on you boys. I'll make a clean breast of it, because I'm just beginning to see how hard you've worked to help me. But please don't be disappointed if I can't tell you much."

"You must know enough to implicate the gang," Frank reminded him. "Otherwise, they wouldn't be so eager to get hold of you again."

To the brothers' surprise, Grafton shook his head. "I don't know as much as they think I do. They never really took me into their full confidence, because I refused to join the gang."

Although disappointed, Frank suggested that

Grafton tell them what he knew. "First, what's their racket? That's the big question."

"I'm not sure. I only have my suspicions. Suppose I start at the beginning. After we crossed the border, Wetherby took me to a lonely hideout, where he had three Mexicans waiting for us. I didn't like the men's looks. All they talked about was making easy money. That's when I became suspicious and said so. But Wetherby wouldn't let me go, and it was then I realized I really was his prisoner.

"Twice we went to town and on threat of death Wetherby made me get his bad personal checks cashed at food stores. He had some checks on a Mexican bank and used an assumed name."

"Did you try to break with him?" Frank asked.

"Yes. But it was hopeless. Wetherby again offered me a share in their illegal racket. When I refused, he set the men to guard me at the lonely spot. After that, they were always careful about what they said. But I did overhear some talk about zinc plates. That makes me think they must be counterfeiters of some kind."

"But what are they counterfeiting?" Frank queried.

"That I don't know."

"Maybe I do!" Joe exclaimed suddenly. "Mr. Grafton, did you ever hear the names of any Americans in the racket?"

"Yes, I did. Al Purdy was one."

Frank and Joe exchanged glances. The handkerchief they had found had the initial P on it!

Frank and Joe almost shouted in their excitement. Joe cried out, "Al Purdy must have been the phony bellman!"

Grafton went on, "Purdy had two buddies Caesar and Ringer."

Quickly the Hardys told Grafton of their own encounters with Purdy, Ringer, and Caesar. "And this same Purdy is the man Chet discovered making a mysterious trip into the desert at night," Joe finished. "And the one who knocked him out in Bayport and stole the prints."

"There's just one thing that doesn't fit into the picture," Frank remarked.

"What's that?" Joe asked.

"The rock we found with the jasper in it. Mr. Grafton, does the gang deal in semiprecious stones? We found a valuable rock near the spot where your plane was abandoned. Could that be what Purdy was looking for when Chet snapped his picture in the desert?"

Perplexed, Grafton shook his head. "I doubt it. I don't remember seeing any such rock myself, and I don't think Purdy had anything to do with it. Probably some rock hunter lost it."

"Then Purdy was here for another reason," Frank declared. "We may have arrived at the right time to make a capture!"

A gentle put-putting sound from up the river

cut short the conversation. Squinting against the glare of the sun upon the water, Joe made out a good-sized motorboat carrying two people.

"Probably Chet and his friend looking for us," he guessed. "I'll run down to the dock and wave."

As a response to Joe's signal, the putting sound swelled to a roar like that of a buzz saw. The boat shot toward the dock, throwing up a white spray on either side of her prow.

A lean, handsome young man, his skin deeply tanned and his blond hair bleached nearly white by the sun, leaped nimbly to the dock to secure the boat. Meanwhile, Chet began passing food supplies to Joe. "Meet Jim Weston. Jim, these are the two mystery hounds I told you about. Frank and Joe Hardy."

The three shook hands. Then each took an armful of packages and walked toward the cabin. Frank and Joe quickly sized up Chet's new friend. Weston appeared to be about twenty-two years old. The brothers liked his firm handshake, and his clear, open gaze.

"Careful!" Chet cried out to Joe. "Those are eggs! And be sure you put this meat in the refrigerator right away!"

"Okay, okay, old lady," Joe retorted.

Watching from the porch, Grafton chuckled. Jim in turn looked startled at the unshaven, poorly dressed old cowboy at the other end of the porch.

"Say," he said in a low voice to the Hardys, "I thought something top secret was going on here."

"I see what you mean." Frank laughed. "That's part of the secret. Jim, meet Willard Grafton, the Los Angeles industrialist!"

Courteously Grafton got up and extended his hand. "How do you do?" The strong grip and the rich, full voice of a younger man puzzled poor Weston all the more.

Smiling, Frank explained. "Mr. Grafton had to change his appearance drastically for his own safety."

After a late, quick lunch, Frank, Joe, and their three companions spent the afternoon discussing the next move. It was concluded that any more daytime operations might make them targets for the enemy. They would wait until evening.

"Suppose I go up tonight and get some shots of the whole area," Jim suggested. "My ship's nearby at the Ripley airstrip, and my developing equipment is there in a garage. If the photos show anything suspicious, we can get back to Blythe or over to Arizona right away to investigate."

"Sounds fine," Frank approved. "Have you room for Joe and me?"

"Sure thing. My ship's a three-seater."

When the afternoon was waning, Chet spoke up on the subject nearest to his heart. "Say, everybody, it's getting toward suppertime. I bought some especially good provisions—"

Joe winked at the others. "Don't mind us, Chet. Start cooking any time."

A gloomy look settled on their chum's round face. "Just when I was hoping for a decent meal. You know I can't cook worth anything. Eating is what I'm good at."

Willard Grafton exploded with laughter. "And I believe you, Chet! I'm not much on eating, myself, but I like to cook. Suppose we make a deal?"

Much to the satisfaction of everyone, Grafton soon proved that he knew food as well as he knew horses and ponies. He gave each person a job to do, and within an hour a tasty spaghetti supper, prepared with Grafton's own special sauce, was on the table.

"Know something?" Frank asked his brother in an undertone as the five friends took a stroll toward the dock. "This is doing Grafton a lot of good. I think he's really enjoying himself. Maybe we can convince him the world is not so bad, if we keep at it."

For some time the whole party had been aware of the drone of an airplane flying nearby. Now the sound suddenly increased to a terrifying, deafening roar as the craft headed toward them. It seemed as if the plane would crash right into the little cabin! But it zoomed away.

"What's that fool doing, buzzing us?" Jim Weston cried angrily.

The ship, a small biplane, started around in a wide, banking turn.

"Looks like one of those crop-dusting crates," Jim said. "Here he comes again!"

"Look out!"

This time the strange aircraft came in trailing a thick, spreading, grayish cloud. The Hardys and their friends raced for the cabin but could not make it. They were enveloped in a blinding, choking chemical fog. They could see nothing, but could hear the mysterious plane roaring in for another pass.

"Hit the dirt!" Frank cried out, and coughing violently, he flung himself to the ground.

Immediately the earth was rocked by a terrific blast. The tinkle of shattered glass mingled with the noise of the airplane as it pulled away.

CHAPTER XVIII

Sleuthing by Camera

FRANK was the first to recover from the shock of the explosion. Holding a handkerchief to his nose, he struggled up and groped his way toward the cabin. Already a light breeze from the river had begun to disperse the fog, and he was able to check the damage. The building had not been hit, but one window had been shattered by the blast.

"Wow! We're in a regular war!" Joe called, joining his brother. "Anything left in here, Frank?"

"That crop-dusting was a smoke screen, so they could bomb us," Jim Weston declared.

"Missed the cabin completely, though," Joe noted. "The explosion seemed closer than it was."

"Out here! This is where it landed!" Chet shouted from the river's edge.

They hurried toward the dock. Frank, Joe, and

Jim discovered that the boards nearest the camp had been crushed like matchsticks. The bomb had also gouged a big hole out of the shoreline, muddying the water all around.

"Good night! The boat!" Frank exclaimed.

"Don't worry," Willard Grafton reassured him. "She's riding fine—didn't even swamp."

Luckily Jim Weston had secured the mooring line to the very end of the dock and the boat was undamaged.

"They must have spotted Jim and me coming down the river this noon," Chet figured. "They tried to kill us while we were all together at the cabin!"

Frank disagreed. "No, their aim couldn't be that bad. More likely they wanted to destroy the boat to keep us off the river. The pilot buzzed the first time to check the boat's position, then laid his smoke screen to cover up what he was about to do and finally dropped his bomb."

"But, in the meantime, the boat had drifted farther from shore," Joe broke in. "It's plain our enemies don't want us to have a boat!"

"Because they don't want us crossing to the Arizona side," his brother added promptly. "This gang has planned some big operation for tonight, and I'm sure the giant over there has something to do with it!"

"Then," Jim Weston spoke up, "the sooner we get to the airstrip the better. That's where those crop-dusting planes operate from normally. Maybe that crop duster took off from there."

"Right," Frank agreed. "As soon as it's dark we'll fly over the effigy in your plane. We'd better get started right away."

"Whoa!" Chet objected. "What about Mr. Grafton and me?"

"Pull in the boat, so it'll be ready when we need it. And keep a sharp lookout for any spies!"

"But suppose they bomb us again?" Chet asked in a worried voice.

"I think they're too busy for that now."

Frank, Joe, and Jim Weston set out for the main road at a brisk walk. Reaching it, they put out their thumbs as a line of cars, already showing lighted head lamps, approached. None of the vehicles stopped for the hitchhikers.

"What a time for a delay!" Joe fumed.

"Let's not give up," Jim advised. "Somebody will take pity on us."

The very next car proved the young pilot to be right. "Hop in, Jim," said a friendly voice. It was a farmer who was a good friend of Weston's. "Where to?"

"Ripley airstrip, Mr. Wells—real fast!"

"Hang on, then!"

As they drove, Jim introduced Frank and Joe and explained that all three were engaged on a secret detective mission.

"Sounds serious. Anything I can do to help?"

"Well, sir," Joe answered for the pilot, "we'll want to go back to our boat in a mighty big hurry."

"Keep my car then, boys," the generous farmer offered. "I can walk home from the airstrip. My house is right near there."

It was completely dark when he and the Hardys reached their destination. The car's headlights picked out a small yellow airplane in front of some low sheds and a gasoline pump.

"That's mine," said Jim briefly, leading the way toward a light in one of the sheds.

"Tomás!" the young pilot called.

The door swung open and an old Mexican, chewing lazily, faced them. "*Sí?* Oh, Jim."

"Any take-offs in the past two hours?"

The old fellow thought a moment. "No, *señor.* Nothing since noon."

"Okay. Now look, Tomás. My friends and I are going up in my ship. Can you light up some flares at the end of the strip a little later, so we'll be able to land?"

The old man nodded agreement. "How long you be gone?"

"Not long—half hour, maybe."

"Good. I go out right now."

Overhead the stars sparkled against a clear, deep-blue sky. The moon had not yet risen. The young sleuths took places inside the little plane and Jim started the engine. The propeller turned over once, twice, then purred in a smooth idle.

Taxiing into the light breeze, Jim gunned his motor and the little ship shot forward into the dark night. Instinctively Frank and Joe gripped their seats.

"Don't need flares on take-off," Jim assured them. "I could get off this strip blindfolded."

It was not until the plane had soared into the air, and the twinkling lights of houses could be seen below, that the Hardy brothers relaxed.

Climbing high, the plane went straight across the river.

Jim said, "Frank, will you take the controls while I get out my infrared camera? As I figure it, we should be over the giants in a few moments."

"You know," said Joe, "I could have sworn the place was lighted up, but it's dark now. Say, I think I see a tiny red light."

"I'll bet it's a signal," Frank agreed excitedly. "But not meant for us, that's for sure!"

"We'll answer it, anyway," said Jim Weston. "Swoop in low, Frank, and I'll shoot with the camera."

"Look! The light's gone. I'd better hurry."

Banking around, and watching his instruments carefully, Frank made a low-level run over the cliff, while Jim took several shots.

"They drop bombs, but we fight with pictures," Joe noted grimly. "Let's see who wins!"

After a second low-altitude pass, Jim took over the controls again and headed back across the

"I'll bet it *is* a signal!" Frank agreed excitedly

river. By this time Tomás had lighted a number of orange kerosene flares to mark the small Ripley airstrip. Jim landed upwind and then taxied back to the sheds.

"My lab is right over here," he told them. "Follow me."

Carrying the exposed plates, the tall pilot led the way to a tiny shack. He unlocked the door and switched on the light in a small but neat darkroom, decorated with a number of fine aerial photographs.

Jim quickly immersed the plates in developing fluid. As soon as the proper time had elapsed, all three crowded around the sink to examine them.

"Here's a man!" said Joe, pointing to one plate. "Near the smaller giant."

"And here are two more!" added Weston. "How about it? Are they familiar? I'm sure this one fellow is the same guy Chet photographed the other night."

"That's the one all right," Joe agreed. "The eavesdropper, the bellman—otherwise known as Al Purdy."

"The other two," said Frank, "are the strong-arm men—Ringer and Caesar. And none of them were running away. They're just standing still."

"Do you think they're waiting for a plane?" Jim Weston asked.

Frank nodded. "No doubt about it. That red light was an unmistakable signal."

"And I'm certain," Joe declared, "that there were other, brighter lights until the men heard us coming. Then they put them out."

Jim looked puzzled. "Nobody could land a plane there, even a helicopter, in the dark. So maybe they do have a lot of lights."

"I'm inclined to think," Frank broke in, "that they're not waiting for someone to land, Jim. They're expecting something to be dropped from a plane!"

"Like what?"

"A shipment of counterfeit United States government checks," Joe answered. "That's this gang's racket, Jim. It's my guess, after hearing about the zinc plates, that Wetherby's gang prints the checks in Mexico, and then smuggles them into this country by air."

"I think it's now or never to capture them," Frank finished.

Jim's face lighted with pleasure. "A fight, you mean? Suits me fine. Let's hear your plan."

"First—back to the cabin. Then the five of us will take the boat about a mile up the river before we cross to the Arizona side. Once over there, we can drift down to the bluff where the big giant is."

"I get you," Jim responded. "That way we won't scare them off."

"Right. How is that bluff, Jim? Can we climb it from the river side in the dark?"

"Sure. It's steep, but we can do it."

"The thing that worries me is the time," Joe put in. "If we don't get there before the shipment is dropped, we'll lose our chance to catch the person or persons who get it."

"Then what are we waiting for?" Quickly Jim removed the plates from the developer and locked his laboratory. Within minutes the three were speeding along the highway in their borrowed automobile.

Turning onto the humpy, gravelly road that led to their cabin, they were forced to slow down. The car's headlights picked out gaping holes and big stones in the road, and the car lurched and bounced a good deal even at low speed.

"Wait!" cried Joe suddenly. "Somebody walking toward us!"

As the jouncing car drew nearer the person, Frank and Joe recognized the heavy-set figure of their friend Chet Morton. Quickly Jim halted.

"Chet!" Joe exclaimed, jumping out. "What's happened? Where are you going?"

"Brr!" the stout boy shuddered, as though he had seen a ghost. "Something weird is going on. There are *two* Mr. Graftons in the cabin!"

CHAPTER XIX

The Attack

"Two Graftons! Talk sense, Chet!" Joe snapped. "We haven't a minute to waste now!"

"S-so help me," the scared Chet stuttered. "I was getting the boat ready, and when I went back into the cabin there were two of them—talking to each other!"

Without waiting to hear more, Frank and Joe set off at a headlong run on a short cut to the cabin. Jim and Chet followed slowly on the rough road in the car.

The black shape of the little cabin loomed in front of the Hardys. Inside, a single kerosene lamp lighted the room dimly. Bursting in, Joe and Frank froze in astonishment. In the flickering shadows stood Willard Grafton, talking to his double.

Slowly, the two figures turned to face the boys.

Both were tall, slim, and unshaven. They wore identical shabby clothes. For one long, ghostly moment they stared mutely at the two youths.

Then abruptly the weird silence was shattered by a familiar laugh from one of them. "Dad!" both boys cried out at the same instant.

"Who did you think I was—Willard Grafton's twin?"

Fenton Hardy and his sons embraced warmly. "Glad to find you both in one piece, boys. Hear you had a little rough play earlier this evening."

"Nothing serious, Dad," Joe replied. "But what a trick for you to play on us! What's the idea, anyhow?"

"If you think you're surprised, you should have seen me," Grafton put in. "I took him for a member of the gang."

The famous detective gave another hearty laugh. "You boys sure cover ground fast. I've been trailing you for days. Up to Colorado, and then back again. Mr. Grafton's friend Redland, the ranch owner, gave me the story. Lent me these clothes and told me just how to disguise myself. I followed you back here and hung around Blythe awhile."

"But why the disguise, Dad?" Joe asked. "Those crooks are out to get Grafton. If they learned about his masquerade, they might have attacked you by mistake."

"Just what I figured," Fenton Hardy admitted. "I was hoping they'd try it, so I could capture them."

Frank, eager not to miss the capture of the suspects across the river, quickly told his father of the necessity of speed. "Let's exchange stories in the boat," he urged.

Mr. Hardy was in agreement. Just then two automobile doors slammed outside. Chet entered the cabin cautiously, followed by Jim Weston.

"Hello, Chet!" the detective boomed. "Where'd you disappear so fast?" he added slyly.

"Mr. Hardy!" Chet exclaimed in astonishment. "Say, that's not fair, sir—to scare a guy so."

After making his peace with Chet and shaking hands with Jim Weston, the detective said he understood the group was about to set off on a mission.

"Tell you all about it in the boat," Frank promised. "But don't talk loudly, anybody. Voices carry across water."

As Jim piloted the motorboat upstream, hugging the California shore, engine quiet and lights out, the brothers briefed their father on the sleuthing they had done. They included details of the recent camera pictures.

"And now tell us your story," Joe begged.

The detective, in a whisper loud enough for them to hear, said, "First, for my case: I've been after a shrewd bunch of counterfeiters of United States government checks, but I haven't caught them yet."

Mr. Hardy took something from his wallet. Cupping one hand over the end of his flashlight, he clicked it on and held the light to a paper. "Chet, is this the kind of check that actor gave you?"

"That's it, all right," the stout boy answered without hesitation.

"Then there's no doubt about it," Fenton Hardy concluded with a little smile. "You three boys and I have been working on the same case from different angles!"

"Tell me, Dad, have you been down in Mexico lately?"

"I *was* down in Mexico, Frank—looking for this gang's printing plant. With some help from the Mexican police I found it, but the ringleaders had vanished. I figured they had fled to the United States, leaving the underlings still working the plant."

"And did you—or did you not—get Joe and me out of jail down there?" Frank interrogated.

Their father chuckled. "I plead guilty."

"But how did you know we were in Mexico?" Joe wondered.

"Your friend Leon Armijo, the station agent, notified the police as soon as you left him, and they relayed his information to me immediately. What made me suspicious was the story of the two Americans in pursuit of the other one. Combing the desert around that lonely station with the Mexican police I came upon the gang's counterfeiting plant."

"So we helped you break the case without knowing it!" Joe declared.

"Yes. I can't seem to get along without you two," their father admitted. "Your method of travel—freight train—even gave me an idea. I thought that might be the way the gang leaders were trying to escape, and I had the border police search all trains."

"And you told them to release us, when caught, and send us on our way," Joe chimed in.

The detective nodded. "I knew you wouldn't have followed the man who escaped unless you were pretty sure he was Willard Grafton. So I went after you, hoping you would find Grafton and he in turn would lead me to the ringleaders.

"The Mexican police are watching the printing plant. They haven't made any arrests yet, because we want to catch the leaders first. I've just had word that a shipment of phony checks is due to go out tonight—to the usual spot in the United States."

"Well, Dad, it's lucky you have your sons to turn to," Joe teased. "We think we've found the place—right where we'll find Mr. Grafton's kidnapers—on the plateau across the river. We think the three men on it are waiting for that package to be dropped from an airplane!"

Fenton Hardy was greatly encouraged by the unexpected news, and as eager as his sons were to capture the men at the effigy, together with the package of incriminating checks.

Joe, impatient, urged that they turn back now and float downstream on the Arizona side. "I hope everybody's ready for a scrap," he said.

"Oh, boy, there are six of us to three," Chet chortled. "But two of them are real tough."

"We'll use the same tactics as last time," Joe told him. "Give them the old football rush."

Mr. Hardy asked Jim Weston if the trip along the cliff would be safe.

"I know this river well," Jim assured the others quietly. "It's illegal not to use lights, of course, but this is an unusual occasion."

"It sure is," Joe agreed. "And a good night to sneak up on those counterfeiters," he remarked from the darkness.

A few minutes later Jim announced, "All right. I'm taking her to the other side."

As they approached the Arizona shore, the black outline of the bluff seemed to loom higher and higher against the stars. Presently Jim cut the motor and they started downstream, without power, hugging the jagged cliff.

The boat drifted silently, with no one speaking.

Occasionally they heard the gentle splash of a fish breaking the surface.

The pilot steered closer to the high, dark bluffs. Then suddenly he stepped overboard with hardly a splash, steadying the boat so the others could climb out easily.

"*Sh!*" he warned. "Mustn't let the bottom scrape. There's a place here to moor her."

Cautiously the party waded ashore, and Jim made the boat fast. When their eyes were accustomed to the new surroundings, the sleuths crossed the narrow beach and began the hundred-foot climb up the rocky cliff.

Jim Weston had made the ascent before, so he led the way. Frank and Joe followed. Then came Chet, while Grafton and Mr. Hardy brought up the rear.

The tricky, dangerous climb seemed to take hours. Any loose rock might cause an avalanche. Even heavy breathing might alarm their enemies and ruin the expedition. So the ascent was slow. At last, however, the rim of the bluff was gained.

Warily Frank and Joe raised their heads above the edge. To their great relief, three black figures were visible against the background of stars.

"Okay." Scarcely breathing the word, Frank reported to the others. By signs, Fenton Hardy indicated that the group should now separate, and take up positions around the edge of the tableland. He himself would give the signal to spring the trap.

Obediently Frank and Joe moved off to the left of their father. When they reached their station, Joe suddenly tapped his brother's shoulder and pointed. Just below them was a cavelike opening in the rock. Frank nodded. A likely hiding place for loot or even counterfeit checks!

Then, at first from far away, came the drone of an airplane. At that instant the plateau was suddenly illuminated. The smaller desert giant was outlined at intervals by lighted lanterns! Three men stood with their backs to the watchers, gazing upward. One was Purdy, but the other two were unfamiliar to the boys.

The plane, flying without lights, circled once above the effigy and then flew away. A vague, puff-like white shape floated down out of the sky.

"A parachute!" Frank breathed.

The shape collapsed on the ground near the giant's elbow and the three men converged on it. Instantly the Hardys and their friends rushed to the attack.

But Frank's and Joe's forward leaps were checked by strong arms that seized them in strangle holds from behind, and covered their mouths with rough palms. Fighting back desperately, the two boys tumbled over and over, locked in combat with their attackers, clear to the bottom of the steep cliff!

CHAPTER XX

Treasure!

STUNNED momentarily by the surprise attack and the fall down the bluff, Frank and Joe felt the struggle going against them. The assailants tightened their choke holds so that the boys could hardly breathe.

"Now," snarled a voice that sounded like Ringer's, "not a sound out of you, if you want to breathe. Listen to what's going on above us, because if the wrong side wins, you two won't live to tell about it!"

Up on the plateau, the attack had gone smoothly. Chet had knocked the wind out of one man with a ferocious football tackle, while rangy Jim Weston had kayoed another with two lightning punches. As the third man turned to flee, he was grabbed by Fenton Hardy and Willard Grafton.

Helpless below the cliff, Frank and Joe heard

their father call out, "That settles them! This gang of counterfeiters has cheated the United States government for the last time!"

Meanwhile, on the cliff, Chet's opponent finally recovered his breath. "Oh-h! They've got us, boss," the Hardy brothers heard him say.

"Shut up, you fool!" barked a thin, shrill voice.

"Wetherby!" cried Grafton. "You were the ring leader!"

"Yes—and I still am!" Menacingly the thin voice went on, "That is, unless Mr. Hardy wants to forfeit his sons' lives in return for my imprisonment."

Startled, Frank and Joe looked at each other.

"Poor Dad!" Frank thought. "It's his duty to capture these men!"

Then came the detective's clear, decisive answer. "You win. I can't fight those conditions. We'll have to turn him loose, Mr. Grafton."

The boys' captors breathed sighs of relief. For a bare instant, their iron grips relaxed.

"Now, Joe!"

Seeing their chance, Frank drove his elbow backward into the solar plexus of his enemy. As the man doubled up, the youth whirled and finished him with a smashing roundhouse blow. Meantime, Joe flipped his assailant over his head. Two sledge-hammer punches kayoed the man.

The boys' escape had taken only seconds. Now, scrambling up the steep cliff, the brothers met one of the gang in the act of stepping down from the rim!

"No, you don't!" Rising up, the boys flung the man back on the tableland.

"We're okay, Dad! Don't let them get away!" Joe cried out.

"Thank goodness for that!" Rushing forward, the detective said their captive was Wetherby and slipped a pair of handcuffs on him. Chet and Jim were guarding Purdy and the stranger.

"The other one looks familiar," Joe said thoughtfully. "I have it—he's the guy we trailed in the motorboat. The one with the bad temper!"

"Well," Frank suggested, "a term in prison should improve his disposition."

"There are two more men down below—out cold," announced Joe. "I think they're Ringer and Caesar."

Mr. Hardy now opened the well-wrapped package dropped from the plane. Hundreds of counterfeit United States government checks dropped out!

"Now we have the evidence!" he exulted.

"Dad," Frank spoke up, "Joe and I have something to show you. Bring your light here a minute."

He guided his father to the cave the boys had noticed earlier. Inside they discovered some digging tools, rope, and another packet of bogus checks.

"We can use this rope," declared Joe as he seized the coil.

Purdy and the boatman stood sullen while their arms were bound behind them. Then the whole party worked its way slowly down the cliff toward the kayoed men. Presently they revived, and were also bound.

The captors were now confronted with a problem; their boat was too small to hold eleven people at one time!

"I'll wait here," Willard Grafton volunteered. "It's the least I can do."

"Stay with him then, Frank and Joe," their father ordered. "You two need a rest after that narrow escape."

"Just a minute!" It was Wetherby's thin, nasal voice. "If you're taking us to the police, you've got to take Grafton too. He belongs to our gang."

"Nonsense!" said Mr. Hardy. "The man's been running away from you for weeks!"

"So what? He worked for us—he passed bad checks for me. Ask him yourself!"

Gloomily Grafton answered, "It's true. I'm ready to face the consequences."

"But he was forced to do what he did, Dad!" Frank and Joe protested warmly.

"A lot of good that will do him," sneered Wetherby. "I'm not licked yet. I'll swear under oath that he and these other guys got me into this thing under force. I'm the innocent one!"

"Why, you dirty double-crosser!" The enraged Purdy turned on his chief. "I'll spill the whole story myself. Grafton's innocent. I'll swear to it, and so will my pals."

"Good," said Mr. Hardy. "Tell your story to the police chief in Blythe. Say, you men must have a boat. Where is it?"

"Hidden near here," Purdy revealed.

Prisoners, sleuths, and their friends crowded into the two boats and the run to Blythe was made. Taxis took the group to police headquarters where the amazed chief listened to the charges.

The detective suggested that Wetherby tell a straight story of the whole counterfeiting project. When he refused, Purdy grudgingly began, "Four months ago me and Wetherby flew over the desert and saw the giants. Wetherby once heard a story that possibly the left arm or leg of one of the figures pointed to treasure, so we started digging. We dug all around in the desert, then on the Arizona bluff. Finally we found gold."

"Gold!" echoed Frank and Joe. "Where?"

"In that little cave you saw tonight. The small giant's leg pointed right to it."

"What kind of gold?" Fenton Hardy asked.

"Old Indian stuff, it was. We were scared to sell it here, so we took it to Mexico. I wanted to split up the money we got, but then Wetherby got a bright idea."

"Which was?" Mr. Hardy prodded.

"To buy a printing press and other equipment and start the racket. The Arizona bluff was a nice out-of-the-way spot, so we decided to have our counterfeit checks dropped there at night. Wetherby rigged up some electric lanterns to outline the giant so our pilot could spot the right place."

"Were you testing the lights tonight a little while before the plane arrived?" Joe asked. "I thought I saw some."

"Yeah. We always did that. We kept the lanterns and battery hid in the cave when we weren't using 'em."

Frank asked, "How did Mr. Grafton happen to come into the picture?"

"Another bright idea of Wetherby's." Purdy snorted in disgust. "He wanted a nice, innocent-looking front man and thought this Grafton would be a sucker to join us. But he wasn't—not even after Wetherby tried to frame Grafton by making him pass some bad checks.

"Then Grafton got away from us," Purdy went on, "and we had to shut him up. That's how I went to Bayport. We thought he'd gone to his uncle's. Then we found out his uncle was calling in you Hardys to find him."

"But somebody tried to warn us on the telephone," Frank reminded him.

Purdy nodded grimly. "One of our boys trying a double cross. I took care of him."

"And then you slugged Chet!"

"That's right." Purdy seemed proud of his work. "I followed you to Chicago in a chartered plane. Got the F.A.A. after you from there, and I was the one who put that note in Grafton's plane. I sneaked in late one night."

"We chased some freight thieves down in Mexico near your plant," Frank said. "Were they in your gang?"

"Nah. We kept our number as small as we could. The Yuma police caught the three Mexicans we had trailing you two, though."

"I suppose you were in the plane that bombed us tonight, too!" Joe accused him.

"That was Caesar," Purdy replied contemptuously. "He made a mess of it—the way this gang made a mess of everything. I should have done the job myself. I was the one that found your cabin. Asked a Mexican farm worker near Ripley. I wish I'd never got into this racket!"

"It was a good racket, you fool," Wetherby burst out, "until it was spoiled by these confounded Hardys!"

"Save it for your trial," the police chief commanded. After he had booked the prisoners, they were untied and led away to cells. The chief now notified the Mexican authorities to close in on the gang who were still in Sonora.

Frank and Joe sighed. Their exciting case was over. But they were soon to plunge into another: **THE CLUE OF THE SCREECHING OWL.**

The Hardys, Chet, Weston, and several police-men stood around in embarrassed silence while Willard Grafton spoke to his wife and two young sons on the telephone. "Yes! Yes!" the happy man assured them eagerly. "I'll fly home tonight in my own plane. I'll leave in less than an hour!

"Now," he told the others after hanging up, "I have one more call to make. Operator, give me Bayport. Mr. Clement Brownlee."

After a pause he said, "Uncle Clement? . . . This is Willard. . . . Yes, I'm all right. I'm not in any trouble—not *now*. I just called to thank you for one thing: you got the Hardy family inter-ested in finding me!"

As the grateful man turned away from the tele-phone to thank Frank, Joe, and Chet, his voice was breaking with emotion. "Boys," he said, "you did more than a great detective job. You educated me. Living with you for these past few days has taught me that there are still plenty of wonderful people in the world.

"I promise you, if I ever get sour on life again, all I'll need to keep up my spirits will be to re-mind myself of Frank and Joe Hardy and Chet Morton—three swell fellows!"

Own the original 58 action-packed

HARDY BOYS MYSTERY STORIES®

In *hardcover* at your local bookseller OR
Call 1-800-788-6262, and start your collection today!

All books priced @ $5.99

1	The Tower Treasure	0-448-08901-7	32	The Crisscross Shadow	0-448-08932-7
2	The House on the Cliff	0-448-08902-5	33	The Yellow Feather Mystery	0-448-08933-5
3	The Secret of the Old Mill	0-448-08903-3	34	The Hooded Hawk Mystery	0-448-08934-3
4	The Missing Chums	0-448-08904-1	35	The Clue in the Embers	0-448-08935-1
5	Hunting for Hidden Gold	0-448-08905-X	36	The Secret of Pirates' Hill	0-448-08936-X
6	The Shore Road Mystery	0-448-08906-8	37	The Ghost at Skeleton Rock	0-448-08937-8
7	The Secret of the Caves	0-448-08907-6	38	Mystery at Devil's Paw	0-448-08938-6
8	The Mystery of Cabin Island	0-448-08908-4	39	The Mystery of the Chinese Junk	0-448-08939-4
9	The Great Airport Mystery	0-448-08909-2	40	Mystery of the Desert Giant	0-448-08940-8
10	What Happened at Midnight	0-448-08910-6	41	The Clue of the Screeching Owl	0-448-08941-6
11	While the Clock Ticked	0-448-08911-4	42	The Viking Symbol Mystery	0-448-08942-4
12	Footprints Under the Window	0-448-08912-2	43	The Mystery of the Aztec Warrior	0-448-08943-2
13	The Mark on the Door	0-448-08913-0	44	The Haunted Fort	0-448-08944-0
14	The Hidden Harbor Mystery	0-448-08914-9	45	The Mystery of the Spiral Bridge	0-448-08945-9
15	The Sinister Signpost	0-448-08915-7	46	The Secret Agent on Flight 101	0-448-08946-7
16	A Figure in Hiding	0-448-08916-5	47	Mystery of the Whale Tattoo	0-448-08947-5
17	The Secret Warning	0-448-08917-3	48	The Arctic Patrol Mystery	0-448-08948-3
18	The Twisted Claw	0-448-08918-1	49	The Bombay Boomerang	0-448-08949-1
19	The Disappearing Floor	0-448-08919-X	50	Danger on Vampire Trail	0-448-08950-5
20	Mystery of the Flying Express	0-448-08920-3	51	The Masked Monkey	0-448-08951-3
21	The Clue of the Broken Blade	0-448-08921-1	52	The Shattered Helmet	0-448-08952-1
22	The Flickering Torch Mystery	0-448-08922-X	53	The Clue of the Hissing Serpent	0-448-08953-X
23	The Melted Coins	0-448-08923-8	54	The Mysterious Caravan	0-448-08954-8
24	The Short-Wave Mystery	0-448-08924-6	55	The Witchmaster's Key	0-448-08955-6
25	The Secret Panel	0-448-08925-4	56	The Jungle Pyramid	0-448-08956-4
26	The Phantom Freighter	0-448-08926-2	57	The Firebird Rocket	0-448-08957-2
27	The Secret of Skull Mountain	0-448-08927-0	58	The Sting of the Scorpion	0-448-08958-0
28	The Sign of the Crooked Arrow	0-448-08928-9			
29	The Secret of the Lost Tunnel	0-448-08929-7		*Also available*	
30	The Wailing Siren Mystery	0-448-08930-0		The Hardy Boys Detective Handbook	0-448-01990-6
31	The Secret of Wildcat Swamp	0-448-08931-9		The Bobbsey Twins of Lakeport	0-448-09071-6

VISIT PENGUIN PUTNAM BOOKS FOR YOUNG READERS ONLINE:
http://www.penguinputnam.com

We accept Visa, Mastercard, and American Express.
Call 1-800-788-6262

Own the original 56 thrilling

NANCY DREW MYSTERY STORIES®

In *hardcover* at your local bookseller OR
Call 1-800-788-6262, and start your collection today!

All books priced @ $5.99

VISIT PENGUIN PUTNAM BOOKS FOR YOUNG READERS ONLINE:
http://www.penguinputnam.com

We accept Visa, Mastercard, and American Express.
Call 1-800-788-6262